Am I in Love?

12 Youth Studies on Guy/Girl Relationships

Karen Dockrey

SAINT LOUIS

All Scripture quotations are taken from the HOLY BIBLE, NEW INTERNATIONAL VERSION®. NIV®. Copyright © 1973, 1978, 1984 by International Bible Society. Used by permission of Zondervan Publishing House. All rights reserved.

Copyright © 1997 Concordia Publishing House
3558 S. Jefferson Avenue, St. Louis, MO 63118-3968
Manufactured in the United States of America

Teachers who purchase this product may reproduce handout pages for use with the lesson plans.

All rights reserved. Except as noted above, no part of this publication may be reproduced, stored in a retrieval system, or transmitted, in any form or by any means, electronic, mechanical, photocopying, recording, or otherwise, without the prior written permission of Concordia Publishing House.

Library of Congress Cataloging-in-Publication Data

Dockrey, Karen, 1955–
    Am I in love? : 12 youth studies on guy/girl relationships / Karen Dockrey.
        p.   cm.
    ISBN 0-570-04979-2
    1. Church group work with teenagers. 2. Teenagers—Religious life. 3. Mate selection—Religious aspects—Christianity—Juvenile literature. 4. Interpersonal relations—Religious aspects—Christianity—Juvenile literature. 5. Love—Religious aspects—Christianity—Juvenile literature. 6. Marriage—Religious aspects—Christianity—Juvenile literature.
    I. Title.
BV4447.D617   1997
241'.6765'0712—dc21   97-5452

---

1   2   3   4   5   6   7   8   9   10   06   05   04   03   02   01   00   99   98   97

Contents

Introduction . . . 5

1. How Do I Know if It's Love? . . . 7
Commit to create love rather than wait for it to fall in your lap.

2. How Can We Get Together? . . . 17
Variety is the spice of love. Together, generate hundreds of ways to get to know one another.

3. What Do I Say? . . . 25
Talking and listening are critical not only in casual conversation but in problem solving, work, play, and more.

4. Is This the One? . . . 33
Love depends much more heavily on mutually choosing to consistently care than on finding a certain someone.

5. Is It Love or Friendship? . . . 41
The best relationships are both/and not either/or. Discover how to grow the best of both friendship and love.

6. Is It Okay to Flirt? . . . 49
Work hand in hand with God to let people honestly know you care. Avoid attracting someone for impure reasons.

7. What if He Doesn't Like Me? . . . 57
Dating worries become good when we turn them into conversations with God and let them become motivation to solve potential problems.

8. How Can I Tell Her I Want to Break Up? . . . 67
Kindly but firmly end relationships that don't have the four pillars of faith, respect, enjoyment, and mutuality.

9. What's the Best Way to Pick a Mate? . . . 75
If dating and breaking up hurt so much, is there a better way?

10. Guys Earn the Money, Girls Keep the House—Or Do They? . . . 85
Look at roles and expectations before you commit to marry each other.

11. Do You Roll or Squeeze the Toothpaste? . . . 93
Discover how to let little things make your marriage rather than break it.

12. We're Ready to Commit—Now What? . . . 101
Work toward a marriage, not just a wedding. Choose actions that cement your relationship while gently prodding growth.

Introduction

The Bible studies in *Am I in Love?* are inviting to youth because they address teenagers' needs and let them talk over their questions with other teenagers. The Bible studies are inviting to leaders because they are complete, Bible-based, and easy to use. Each Bible study demonstrates that God is intimately interested in guy/girl relationships and is the best romance counselor. He wants to be and is uniquely able to work hand-in-hand with youth to design strong friendships, happy romances, and lasting marriages.

Certainly 12 sessions seems like a lot. And even though guy/girl relationships dominate youth's thinking, your youth may tire of the subject after four or five studies. That's precisely the beauty of this series. It's not a one-time-and-its-over type of study. Instead it provides all-new material on guy/girl relationships for several consecutive years. Each year as you choose the subjects youth want to study, romance will be on the list. Rather than repeat the same old studies or search for something new, you'll have up to 12 fresh sessions, each with a unique and deeply Bible-based truth to communicate. You'll equip your teenagers to build love relationships that last a lifetime.

You may find that your youth want to study all 12 sessions at once. There's little more intensely felt need among teenagers than guy/girl relationships. If so, I recommend studying four sessions, breaking for a week or two, then studying four more. Each foursome is loosely connected to a general theme and in an order that builds toward that theme:

- 1–4: The Nature of Love
- 5–8: How to Build True Love
- 9–12: How to Make Marriage Great

At the same time, each session is a stand-alone unit that focuses on a single Goal Truth and can be studied in any order or combination. As you know, your youth group is seldom the same from week to week. Visitors come, regulars go to sports practices, teachers have to miss for illness or family commitments. So you want a session that can be studied in its entirety during a single gathering. The dual nature of *Am I in Love?* provides this: Stand-alone sessions that cooperate beautifully with one another.

Why a series on love, romance, and marriage? Because teenagers think about it almost continually.

- What do I say?
- What if she thinks I'm dumb?
- Why won't he talk to me?
- If it feels so right, how can it be wrong?
- Is it love or friendship?
- Is she the one?
- Can I be happy with him?

Relationships are foundational to everything youth do, yet youth have very little training in them. As a result, young people make life-impacting decisions based on feelings and hope, rather than on facts and character. In the process, youth worry about guy/girl relationships, agonize over them, find joy in them, and find despair in them. These sessions help teenagers turn worry into preparation, agony into solid choices, and despair into caring action.

Even though youth are intensely interested in relationships, they don't always find them easy to talk about. These studies ease youth's hesitance with a variety of learning methods. *Am I in Love?* will guide youth to practice relationship skills in interesting ways including communication strategies, problem-solving skills, games to discover if a certain guy/girl is "right," unique listing processes for thinking of things to say, ways to express commitment, talk translation, wedding planning, and more. These skills help youth make their own smart choices rather than just let friendship, romance, and marriage happen or not happen to them.

Assure your students that love is a choice, not a chance. Youth don't have to wait for Mr. or Miss. Right to come along, nor do they have to settle for less than a good match. Youth can make choices and take action to create happy relationships. In the meantime, they can enjoy life. The Bible studies in *Am I in Love?* show them how.

Features

Is This the One?
Each title is a question youth often ask.

2 Corinthians 6:14–16; Galatians 5:22–23
Each session is based in Scripture.

Focus on a Goal Truth
Your trying to teach too much results in their learning too little. But when you focus on a single truth and repeat it a different way in every step, youth go out of the session firmly understanding that truth.

Understand Concerns Youth Have
Youth seek Bible answers, but they don't always realize it. These concerns summarize what youth are thinking and asking.

Connect Scripture to Youth Concerns
This section draws the correlation between the Bible and youth's concerns. These opening statements are an abbreviated version of the session so you can see at a glance what you'll be doing.

Gather Supplies and Prepare
Supplies and extra preparation are listed in the order you will need them.

Invite Attention
This step hooks youth interest, prompting them to focus closely on the Scripture and how it impacts them.

Dig into the Bible
This step guides youth to open and learn their Bibles so they can apply Scripture in subsequent steps.

Live What You Learn
Though all steps relate to teenagers' lives, this step focuses most heavily on application of the Bible truth youth have experienced.

(10 minutes)
Suggested time increments are provided with each step. Each session lasts 50–60 minutes. Because your group will spend more time on some steps and less on others, these can seldom be exact. Sometimes your group will get so involved in one step that you don't have time to do all five steps. That's okay. Do the first and final steps and then do the other steps as time allows. Most sessions include more than enough to do in an hour so use what will work with your group.

Handout
One or two reproducible pages enhance your teaching in each session. Quite different from standard worksheets, these include cubes to discuss, puzzles to manipulate, pamphlets to design, and games to strategize.

Bonus Option
This option uses more materials or a different approach to teach the same truth. Let it replace one or more of your steps or serve as an advertisement or introduction to a session.

Teacher Tip
Teaching youth calls for customized skills. This tip gives a tone, strategy, or question technique that increases learning.

Delight in studying guy/girl relationships with your teenagers (Matthew 6:33).

1 Corinthians 13:4–7; Genesis 2:24–25

SESSION 1

How Do I Know if It's Love?

Focus on a Goal Truth

Love is a creation more than a discovery.

Understand Concerns Youth Have

- Am I in love?
- When will I find someone I like?
- How can I know if my love will last?

Connect Scripture to Youth Concerns

1. Examine current ideas about love by making a greeting card.
2. Discover Bible actions that create true love by making a switch puzzle.
3. Evaluate the level of my love through 60-second speeches and report cards.

Gather Supplies and Prepare

- Bring extra Bibles, paper in a variety of colors, marking pens, and masking tape.
- Photocopy Handout 1 for Step 2. As students enter, let each fold a handout.
- Write the 10 questions on question marks for Step 3.
- Photocopy Handout 2 for Step 5. Bring pencils.
- Bring paper to write letters if you choose the Bonus Option.

SESSION 1

Bonus Option

Invite youth to name someone's marriage they want to imitate. Insist that this be someone they see regularly rather than a star or someone they've merely read about. Guide youth to write that couple thanking them for being a model of marital love.

Invite Attention

Step 1: Show What Love Looks Like (5–10 minutes)

As the youth enter, point out the colored paper, marking pens, masking tape, and pencils. Direct them, **Make a greeting card that shows what true love is. Your picture of love can include symbols, words, or 3-D items made from paper and taped to the card. It can be torn into a symbol; it can apply meaning to a particular color; it can be a combination of all of these.** Circulate and encourage youth as they work, highlighting a specific idea in each such as: Love is forever. Love brings out the best in a man and woman. Love is listening. Love is understanding.

Explain, **I'm going to ask each of you to name a characteristic of real love shown in your card. To show how smart each speaker is, the rest of you will name three places the speaker may have learned this characteristic.** Ask each youth in turn to name a characteristic and three others to name the source of this characteristic. (Sample: "Love is happily ever after" comes from romance novels, fairy tales, magazines.) Ask, **Which sources we named are reliable? Where is the best place to find out if you're in love?** Stress that the Bible, books and magazines that apply the Bible, and Christians who love each other in marriage are places to go for reliable information on love.

Using youth's examples, highlight, **Love is plagued by powerful myths. During this session we'll discover which parts of our cards are based in myth and which are based in truth. We'll discover how to know if you're in love, in like, or in confusion.**

Dig into the Bible

Step 2: Move from Luck to Action (15–20 minutes)

Give each youth a copy of Handout 1. They will probably know how to fold this puzzle, but for adults who may have forgotten: Fold each corner to the center twice so the words *Protects, Trusts, Hopes, Perseveres* show on the outside. Then fold the puzzle in half to make a rectangle, and repeat in the other direction to make the puzzle flexible. Put four fingers in the open flaps on the underside and pinch inward. Say, **To find what real love is, fold this puzzle and then do the switch process with a partner.**

SESSION 1

This will help you discover key qualities of true love from 1 Corinthians 13. To switch the puzzle pick a word on the outer flap and make one switch for each letter of the word. Then pick an inner word (or phrase) and make one switch for each letter of that word (or phrase). Finally select a flap and open it to find the definition of that love quality. Guide youth to keep playing until they discover the definitions for all eight love qualities. All definitions are adapted from the *Holman Student Bible Dictionary* (Broadman and Holman, 1993).

After youth finish, point out that working this puzzle has settled the meaning of real love in our minds and hearts. Invite each youth to name one of the eight love qualities and give an example of it based on its definition (Patient, Kind, Does Not Envy, Does Not Boast, Not Proud, Not Rude, Not Self-seeking, Not Easily Angered, Keeps No Record of Wrongs).

Draw attention to the four words on the outside of the puzzle and explain that true love also does these things: *Protects, Trusts, Hopes, Perseveres.* Invite each youth to put all four words in a sentence about love. (Sample: True love *trusts* the other by protecting treasured dreams, *hoping* and working together to make those trusted dreams come true, *protecting* feelings by speaking honestly but kindly, and *persevering* together through tough times.)

Review, **Where do these characteristics of love come from?** (1 Corinthians 13:4–5.) Invite youth to look in their Bibles to name the two qualities in verse 6 that summarize those in verses 4–5. (Does not delight in evil, rejoices with the truth.) Then invite volunteers to name a time they failed this verse 6 test. (Samples: I was proud when I was right and my boyfriend was wrong. I was secretly glad when my sister got in trouble.)

Discuss 1 Corinthians 13:4–7 with the following:

1. **What love quality has the most power to build true love, in your experience?** (Urge each youth to choose a different quality or at least give different reasons for each quality.)
2. **How is the puzzle itself like and unlike true love?** (Samples: Unlike the puzzle, love is not something you just open and find, but it is something you create. Like the puzzle, love is a choice. Like the puzzle you can switch if you see that something needs changing.)
3. **How will you "switch" your view of love, similar to the way you switched the puzzle?** (Samples: I'll deliberately do loving actions. I'll see people who show love already rather than look to fall in love. When I see a fall-in-love image, I'll switch it to a love-is-a-choice image.)
4. **Why is love more a choice than a feeling?** (Samples: Feelings come and go, love can be forever. Actions are a true indicator of love. All the 1 Corinthians 13 qualities are choices.)

Teacher Tip

Most youth assume that love is something they find or fall into. Notice how the switch puzzle moves them from magical thinking to love-is-something-you-create. Use several aspects of the puzzle to do this:

Switch: We can deliberately switch from myths to truth by paying attention to what movies, music, books, and television say about love. Then we can sort truth from fiction.

Fake Fortune: Switch puzzles are sometimes used to pretend to tell the future. But love is much more a choice than a destiny.

Bible Truth: The love qualities in this puzzle come from the Bible, the source of truth for everyday living.

SESSION 1

Step 3:
How Do I Know if I'm in Love?
(15 minutes)

Say, **Even though you know that love is purposeful and that love is for friendships and acquaintances, you still want to know how to recognize love with that special someone. Here are 10 questions you can ask yourself to discover the answer. Also ask others to watch your relationship for the answers. I'll give you the questions and you speak to the group as the love authority.** Photocopy and cut apart the following paragraphs. Tape each to the back of a separate construction paper question mark, and give one question-plus-paragraph to each of 10 youth. If you have more than 10 youth, assign more youth to each question. If fewer than 10, assign more than one question to each youth. Then invite each youth to speak for 60 seconds on how that question tells about love, adding an example he or she has seen. Ask the others to take notes.

Love Question 1: *Do we bring out the best in each other?* True love brings out more of your good qualities than your bad. You don't have to hide anything or hesitate to share certain parts of your personality. True love frees you to turn to God rather than feel you must hide your commitment to Him. True love helps you be your best rather than press you into how your date expects you to act. True love commits to help the other be his or her best. Invite friends and family members to tell you how you've changed since you've been dating. If the change is positive, you may have built love.

Love Question 2: *Do we share the same beliefs and goals?* True love does not compete with your convictions; it makes them stronger. True love talks openly about God and about how to serve Him. The closest couples agree in their understanding of God and they encourage each other to live those beliefs. You don't have to "wait until he or she is in a good mood" to talk about matters of faith. It's a part of everyday conversation. If the two of you avoid talking about religion or faith, you haven't found true love.

Love Question 3: *Do we know each other?* The longer you've been friends and the longer you've dated, the less chance you have to be surprised after marriage. We've all heard stories of waking up to a different person after the honeymoon—know each other well to prevent this. Spend time with each other's families. Watch how your date treats other people. Watch how he or she treats and talks about babies, kids, peers, parents, and senior adults. Notice each other's strong and weak qualities, and how those qualities impact daily life. Invite friends and family members to tell what they see too. Those in love know each other well and like well what they know.

Love Question 4: *Is school/work/family going well?* True love motivates you to do better in every area of life. When you are happily in love, you'll make better grades, you'll concentrate better at work, you'll get along better with friends and family. You'll also be more excited about reaching your goals. If you give up an education, a passion, a dream for the relationship, it's likely not love. True love prompts you to reach your dreams, work for education, excel in your skill. If you find yourself preoccupied or unable to concentrate, you've not yet developed mature love. But if you study together, ask each other about work, and motivate each other to do well, you may have found love.

Love Question 5: *Can we work together?* Encouraging each other in the basic efforts of life is the core of marital happiness. True love makes the mundane marvelous. Day-to-day tasks become fun when you do them with someone you love. Do you cooperate? Do you compliment rather than pout when he or she does better than you did? Can you take instructions from each other? Can you do chores together? These are important love skills.

Love Question 6: *Are our relationships with other people better?* True love makes it easier to get along with everyone in your life: family, friends, church members, teammates, enemies. If your other relationships are strained or neglected, you have obsession not love. One who truly loves you will get to know the people in your life, grow to love them, help you communicate with them, and will want you to spend time with them. Of course some family relationships may be strained already, but love should make even those easier to manage. If friends and family members have a funny feeling about your romance, listen. They may be wrong, but they're more likely seeing something you're missing.

Love Question 7: *Do we demonstrate respect and admiration for each other?* True love shows itself in action. Does he include you in conversations even when his friends are around? Do you show affection for one another besides physically? Does she listen to and consider your ideas? Is he willing to learn from you? Does she show excitement over your accomplishments? Does he show sensitivity to your moods and needs? Does she proudly introduce you to friends and family? Does he know just what to say to help you feel good? These examples of steadily shown care indicate that true love may be present.

SESSION 1

Love Question 8: *Do we trust each other?* Jealousy may seem romantic, but it demonstrates a lack of personal security. This can lead to possessiveness, abuse, stalking, and refusal to let your loved one live life. True love gives the other person freedom, knowing that only in freedom can true love grow. Then as that love grows, confidence that the other cares makes trust even easier. You don't have to worry when a potential competitor comes along because your relationship has a solid foundation. True love gives the other person freedom to spend time alone and with friends. True love gives freedom to think for yourself and to motivate yourself to do the right thing.

Love Question 9: *Do we both give equally to the relationship?* True love is mutual. Each person does some of the giving and some of the receiving. This is not a 50/50, score-keeping thing (see *keeps no record of wrongs* in 1 Corinthians 13:5) but a 100 percent/100 percent commitment. Each is willing to give his or her all to the relationship whenever it is needed. On those days when she faces a huge decision, he does almost all the listening. Next time she'll do the same for him. On typical days, each listens and speaks about as much as the other. Each brags about the other. Each takes turns doing what the other wants to do. Each learns to detect the other's feelings and ask about them. When one does most of the giving or most of the talking, it's using, not love.

Love Question 10: *Can we solve problems?* Problems come to every life. True love faces those problems head on, finds possible solutions, picks the one that will work, and patiently implements it. Only an ostrich with its head in the sand would assume that love erases all problems. The rest of us recognize that love means facing problems and that true love will do whatever needs to be done with a patient persistence. Are you willing to swallow your pride, or do you attack each other when the going gets rough? Do you negotiate or demand your way? Do you consider the other's needs and feelings or assume your needs and feelings come first? Do you attack the problem or attack each other? True love effectively and directly solves problems.

Step 4: Work toward Forever (5 minutes)

Emphasize, **Ultimately love is a commitment to stay with each other through thick and thin, to consciously work to bring out the good in the other, to deliberately show interest in the other's experiences and goals.** The Bible teaches this from the first book to the last. Ask a youth to read Genesis 2:24–25. Invite youth to share how one of the 10 questions or the 12 love characteristics from 1 Corinthians 13 will create a lifelong love.

Live What You Learn

Step 5: Grade Your Love
(10 minutes)

Recall the 12 love characteristics from 1 Corinthians 13 that we've been discussing. Explain to the students that 1 Corinthians 13 is a treatise on God's love for us in Jesus Christ. The focus of 1 Corinthians 12 is gifts of the Spirit exercised lovingly in the body of Christ. Discuss the application of 1 Corinthians 12 with your students as you work through this step. Invite volunteers to recite as many of the love characteristics from 1 Corinthians 13 as they can. Congratulate all efforts. Then give each youth a copy of Handout 2 and direct them to grade themselves or a relationship on the 12 characteristics, giving at least one example for each. ("I get a/n _____ on patience when I_____.") If they grade a relationship, direct them to grade each person in the relationship on each of the 12 characteristics. If both members of a couple are in your group, consider letting them grade the relationship independently and then subtly compare. Direct youth to score themselves on whether they think they're in love, in like, or in confusion and why.

Invite youth to share one love characteristic in which they make a high grade and one in which they need to raise their grade. Say, **Ultimately love is a commitment to choose to do the caring action. Watch for signs of this kind of commitment in the people you date. You'll see it in the 12 love characteristics.** Assure youth that God will guide them to love in His good time or will guide them to be content as singles. Stress, **Now that we know that love is more a choice than a discovery, let's spend a few weeks discovering how to make those choices.** Urge youth to attend the other sessions in this study.

SESSION 1 — HANDOUT 1

Switch Puzzle

Photocopy this sheet. Tear off this instruction flap and then fold this puzzle like when you made switch puzzles in elementary school. As you work the puzzle, ponder why true love is more than good fortune. Why is it something you create rather than something you fall into?

HOPES

Kind

Patient

TRUSTS

Does Not Envy

Kind: Good-hearted, gentle, friendly, generous, willing to feel another's feelings and understand.

Patient: Longsuffering or enduring; choosing to be kind even when times are tough.

Keeps No Record of Wrongs

Does Not Envy: Is not jealous, does not covet or want greedily what another has. True love has no need to compete.

Keeps No Record of Wrongs: Love talks about problems when they arise rather than waiting to use past wrongs as ammunition.

Not Proud and Does Not Boast: Bragging and calling attention to self have no place in true love. True love happens between two secure people.

Not Easily Angered: Anger is a good emotion when used against evil, but quick anger is usually self-centered and ugly.

Not Proud and Does Not Boast

Not Easily Angered

Not Rude: Love is hurt when lovers are coarse, contemptuous, ugly. Real love kindly considers the other's feelings.

Not Self-seeking: Selfish people expect the world to revolve around them. They hurt people by saying and doing demanding things.

PERSEVERES

Not Rude

Not Self-seeking

PROTECTS

14

HANDOUT 2 — SESSION 1

Love Report Card

How does God's Holy Spirit help you live out each love characteristic? Give yourself a grade from A to F on each love characteristic, including evidence of how both you and the one you like express it to each other.

Love Report Card

_____ 1. *Patient.* Evidence:

_____ 2. *Kind.* Evidence:

_____ 3. *Does Not Envy.* Evidence:

_____ 4. *Does Not Boast and Not Proud.* Evidence:

_____ 5. *Not Rude.* Evidence:

_____ 6. *Not Self-seeking.* Evidence:

_____ 7. *Not Easily Angered.* Evidence:

_____ 8. *Keeps No Record of Wrongs.* Evidence:

_____ 9. *Protects.* Evidence:

_____ 10. *Trusts.* Evidence:

_____ 11. *Hopes.* Evidence:

_____ 12. *Perseveres.* Evidence:

Give each A a score of 4, B a score of 3, C a score of 2, D a score of 1, and F a score of 0. Add up your score.

1–23 means confusion. Your relationship either needs more experience to see the good or, more likely, you need to flee this relationship.

24–35 means you're in definite like. Raise each grade to at least a B before getting serious.

36–48 means your relationship has the potential for lifetime love. Keep working to bring your grades up to A.

Romans 12:1–2, 9–21

SESSION 2

How Can We Get Together?

Focus on a Goal Truth

Variety is the spice of togetherness, a feeling of oneness and on-the-same-team-ness. The more different settings you see your date in, the better you'll discover whether togetherness can grow.

Understand Concerns Youth Have

- How can I know if this is the one?
- We're bored with each other. How can we keep our relationship interesting?
- There's nothing to do in this town.

Connect Scripture to Youth Concerns

1. List at least 26 different dates that build togetherness.
2. Examine specific actions that build togetherness whether on a date or not.
3. Compose a brochure that shows how to build togetherness that lasts.

Gather Supplies and Prepare

- Bring extra Bibles, pencils, and masking tape.
- Bring paper with the alphabet typed down the left side. Create the page on a computer or word processor or invite a youth to draw it. Then photocopy.
- Photocopy Handout 3.
- Tape paper to the wall for Step 2.

SESSION 2

- Cut enough small slips of paper for each student. Write *Spontaneous* on half the slips and *Deliberate* on the other half. Put all the slips in one envelope to be used in Step 3.
- Bring spices for Step 4 or post a list of at least 10 spices.
- Fold 8½ × 11 papers in thirds to form pamphlets. Prepare one for every youth to allow extras if youth work in pairs. This is for Step 5.
- Invite couples and compose questions if you choose the Bonus Option.

Invite Attention

Step 1: List Tons of Togetherness Dates (10 minutes)

As youth enter, say, **One of the best indicators of true love is enjoying each other when you're together. I challenge you to name for every letter of the alphabet a way to have fun with someone you like,** *besides* **kissing and hugging.** Distribute Handout 3. Say, **This handout will give you some starter ideas; you can use up to 10 ideas from it.** (Other ideas: **A**ppreciation expressed—"I like the way you always listen"; **B**roach hard-to-talk-about subjects; **C**an share everyday stuff such as chores; **D**iscipline yourself to say the kind word; … **Z**ip your lip when you want to gossip; instead tell the good about people.)

Ask each youth around the room to name ideas for each letter. Applaud generously after each letter. Say, **You have given some great ideas for growing love. A mark of true love is togetherness, a feeling of oneness and on-the-same-team-ness. How can you know if your relationship has true togetherness?** Using youth's comments help them see that the more settings they see their date in, and the more people they see their date with, the better they can see if they're compatible. Time together helps us know each other, which helps us build togetherness or see that togetherness is unlikely with this person.

Add, **In the best relationships, people are together emotionally, spiritually, socially, and intellectually. But too many relationships deteriorate to the physical only because couples don't know what else to do together. You have given yourself advice that can keep this from happening in your relationships—by doing the variety of dates you've suggested, you can build a relationship that's close in every way: spiritually, emotionally, intellectually, and socially.** (Explain that "socially" encompasses acquaintances and close friendships.) Ask, **Why is**

variety the spice of love? Invite youth to tell how they liked somebody better by doing something new together.

Explain that togetherness is more than just a bonus, it's a measure of how strong the relationship can be. Say, **The more different things you do together and the more different circumstances you see each other in, the better you can see if your relationship will last.**

Dig into the Bible

Step 2: Implement Togetherness Actions (10–15 minutes)

Point out, **When we're dating, getting together is a big event, something you plan for all week, or at least for several hours. But because life is mostly made up of routine things such as school, work, and chores, those with true togetherness can make these as eventful as dates. Let's find out how.** Direct youth to turn in their Bibles to Romans 12:9–21. Wait until all find it and then explain, **In Romans 8, Paul talks about relationships within the body of Christ. We can apply these same love-building actions to all our relationships. The key to true togetherness is seeing every conversation and every encounter as a chance to grow close. Romans 12:9–21 offers more then 20 ways to grow close. I'll give you 90 seconds to find these ways and give an example for each.** Point out the paper you have taped to the wall. Generate enthusiasm, **When I say go, run to the paper on the wall and list ways and examples. Up to two of you can work together.** Wait briefly so youth can gather their Bibles, pencils, and excitement. Then say **Go!** Give warnings when youth are down to 23 seconds, 13 seconds, and 3 seconds. Then call **Pencils up!** to halt everyone at the same time. Youth will likely want to keep writing; consider giving another 30 seconds. Then stop and congratulate them on their work. Highlight how quickly they found good answers, and stress that they can read and understand their own Bibles.

Invite each youth to name a love-building action from Romans 12:9–21 and an example. (Possibilities include the following: "Be sincere" means I won't lie to my date. "Be devoted" means I will be there when I say I will, even if something else comes up. "Keep your spiritual fervor" means I will be kind even when I'm in a grouchy mood because God reminds me this is the right thing to do. "Do not be proud" means I will admit it when I'm wrong, or could be wrong. "Be careful to do what is right in the eyes of everybody" reminds me to consider friends' and family's evaluation of my

SESSION 2

Teacher Tip

Because youth need the information on the worksheet to help with their alphabet lists, they are more likely to read every word of it.

SESSION 2

Teacher Tip

The racing element makes youth want to do well at this Bible study and want to do it quickly. They race not only against the clock for 90 seconds but against one another to write the most ideas. This is a positive use of competition where everyone becomes a winner in Bible knowledge.

relationship. "Overcome evil with good" means I will replace my bad attitude with a good one.)

Explain, **Love is an action, a choice, a deliberate caring. All this is summarized in Romans 12:1–2. Who will read it? The rest of you listen to put these verses in your own words.** After one youth reads the passage and the others respond, use their words to stress that we give ourselves to God as a "living sacrifice," meaning every word and action is dedicated to God. Loving people is an important way to show our dedication to God. Invite youth to name examples of how friends or dates love them like God loves them.

Direct youth to bow their heads while you lead a prayer inviting God to show each person in the room how to grow in togetherness through deliberate love. Call for volunteers to add a sentence to the prayer, perhaps inviting courage to go with their willingness.

Step 3:
Debate Planned Love and Spontaneous Love
(5 minutes)

Ask, **If you love on purpose, is it love? Isn't love supposed to be spontaneous?** After hearing a few ideas, guide youth to briefly debate whether love is deliberate or spontaneous. Get out the envelope you prepared and guide youth to choose one slip from it without looking. The slips they draw determine their teams. Give a minute to prepare, a minute to each side to present, and 30 seconds to each side to rebut. Using youth comments stress, **Both spontaneity and deliberate action are parts of love. Don't leave either one out or you will shortchange yourself. God had a plan when He came to earth in the person Jesus Christ and His plan showed love. Planning to tell a loved one what you appreciated about the conversation you had is just as loving as if the compliment popped out.** Invite other youth examples. Stress, **Spontaneous love is a good part of love, but it alone can't keep a relationship going. Build both planned and spontaneous love, with the purpose of offering yourselves to God as vehicles of His love.**

Step 4:
Show How Variety Builds Togetherness
(10 minutes)

Help youth continue to debunk the myth that love just happens by letting them illustrate how togetherness grows. Review, **The more places you see each other, and the more people you see each other with, the better you can evaluate how well you love each other. Why is variety the spice of togetherness?** To answer this question direct youth to name a real spice and show how it is like togetherness. Make this easier by bringing a variety of spices from home or post a list of at least 10 spices. Possible answers include

- Togetherness is like *pepper* because it adds flavor to every part of life, but too much togetherness and neglect of other relationships makes you sneeze.
- Togetherness is like *cinnamon* because as cinnamon and sugar taste best together, two people make a great topping to life.
- Togetherness is also like *cinnamon* because just as cinnamon adds flavor to many different recipes, seeing each other in many different settings adds flavor to the togetherness.
- Togetherness is like *basil* and *oregano* because it spices up the pizza of life. Some people run from togetherness just like some don't like *basil* and *oregano*. I'll avoid dating people who won't build togetherness with me.
- Togetherness is like a *bay leaf* because it tastes best when given a little time to simmer. Then the flavor of all you've done together permeates all of life.

Live What You Learn

Step 5: Compose a Togetherness Brochure (15–20 minutes)

To prepare youth to record what they've discovered about building togetherness, stress, **Togetherness is something you build over time. You can't instantly fall in love, but you can build on the instant attraction that may mean you're meant for each other. Let's create a brochure with tips for building togetherness that lasts. But first, let's play a game to generate ideas. Sit in a circle. We'll play three rounds:**

First round: **The person to my left names a way *not* to build togetherness, such as spend all your time together. The person to her left names another way *not* to build togetherness within 10 seconds. If he can't name one, he stands until the next round. All suggestions must differ from one another.** Take time to play this round and to highlight that actions such as criticism and selfishness definitely damage togetherness.

Second round: **The person to my right names a way *to* build togetherness, such as listen to the events of your friend's day. The person to his left names another way *to* build togetherness within 10 seconds. If she can't name one, she stands until the next round. All sug-

Bonus Option

Invite couples from your church who have been married between 10–30 years to serve as a panel on togetherness-building. Request that each couple speak for about a minute on how they have built togetherness over the years. Then open the floor to youth questions. Plant these questions among youth to get discussion going:

- When you were dating, how did you know you were right for each other?
- What's the most unusual date you had and what did it teach you about each other?
- What dating advice do you have for us?
- How do you keep your love alive?

SESSION 2

gestions must differ from one another. Take time to play this round and to stress that intentional care builds togetherness.

Third round: **The person directly across from me says a sentence or word that would invite togetherness such as "What was the best and worst of your day?" or "smart idea." The person to her left must name another invitation line. If he can't name one within 10 seconds, he stands until the end. Each talk invitation must be different.** Take time to play this round and to say that talking and listening are two of the main skills for togetherness-building. Tell students that you'll study these skills next week.

Time the youth as they give ideas, keeping in mind that the 10-second limit and the different-from-the-previous-ideas rule encourages attention and quick idea listing. Use the time limit to keep the game moving, but don't let it make the game unpleasant. After the third round walk around the room to drop folded pamphlet papers ($8^1/_2 \times 11$ papers folded in thirds) at intervals around the edge of the room and say, **When I say go, trios of you gather around the walls where I've laid the pamphlet papers. On one panel, write all the *do's* you think best build togetherness. On one panel write all the *don'ts* that kill togetherness. On a third panel write talk invitations. Design the fourth panel with the information or illustration you think will most help someone grow close to that special person.** Pause to watch youth build anticipation. Then say **Go!**

Note that youth might arrange their pamphlets horizontally or vertically. Ideas for the fourth panel include a Bible verse motto, a diagram of steps to growing together, an illustration that makes youth want to open the brochure. Encourage variety in the brochures, generously praising at least one wise idea in each brochure.

Direct youth to tape their brochures to the wall, and highlight one point in each. Consider photocopying each brochure so youth can both learn from them and give them to friends. Announce that copies will be ready at the next session. Thank the youth for discovering ways to grow Christlike togetherness. Urge them to live what they have learned.

HANDOUT 3 — SESSION 2

Togetherness-Growing Dates

The standard go-out-to-a-movie date doesn't teach you much about each other besides how you like your popcorn. Notice how much you can learn about each other with a variety of dates. Try these to grow real togetherness:

1. **Cook a meal together.** How do each of you make a humdrum task fun? With what kind of attitude do you cook and clean up? This date practices the real-life skill of buying and preparing food. Consider setting a certain amount of money and spending exactly that amount. (Have you ever purchased one grape to spend that last few cents?)

2. **Study together.** What work habits does your date have? How important is school to you? to him or her? How well can you help each other without defensiveness or condescension? What strategies can you discover for managing tough subjects? (You'll need that skill in almost every job!)

3. **Grow a garden.** How well do each of you stick with a long-term project? How do you mark little bits of success along the way? How well do you nurture tiny growing plants? How well do you cooperate?

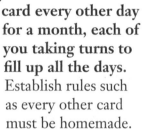

4. **Have a card volley: Give each other a card every other day for a month, each of you taking turns to fill up all the days.** Establish rules such as every other card must be homemade. This is a fun way to express your feelings for each other and it shows how well you put into words the specific things you like.

• •

5. **Try 50+ more ideas suggested by real youth.** Notice what each teaches you about the other: Work a jigsaw puzzle. Go to the planetarium. Attend a Christian concert. Play miniature golf. Exercise together. Share a picnic. Spend an evening with each other's parents. Borrow a kid and take her to the park. Make popcorn. Talk. Tour the city. Cut each other's hair. Choose and read the same library book. Find constellations. Visit a shut-in. Volunteer in Bible school. Play racquetball. Play tennis. Play ping-pong. Attend church activities. Swim. Gather a group for food at your house. Take a long walk. Ride bicycles. Ski. Ice skate. Play hockey. Shoot baskets. Watch each other's ball games. Bowl. Play football. Boat. Play a mystery game with six to eight people. Hear a Christian speaker. Play croquet. Play computer games. Send e-mail to each other. Attend a play. Attend an opera and then try to imitate the singers when you're back home. Tutor a child or a peer. Ride horses. Program a computer. Fish. Go to the zoo. Attend the circus. Play card games. Play board games. Visit relatives. Clean each other's house (with adults in the house). Attend a recital. Go to a car show. Take sailing lessons. Look at clouds and tell the shapes you see.

Ephesians 4:17–19, 25–32

SESSION 3

What Do I Say?

Focus on a Goal Truth

Talking and listening are two critical skills to building a relationship. They are critical not only in casual conversation but in problem solving, work, play, and more.

Understand Concerns Youth Have

- I don't know what to say to her.
- I can't say how I really feel—what if she thinks my dreams are dumb?
- He never quits talking.

Connect Scripture to Youth Concerns

1. Examine ways to listen and speak.
2. Write recipes for tasty communication based on Ephesians 4:17–19, 25–32.
3. Practice listening using the acronym ME HELP.

Gather Supplies and Prepare

- Bring extra Bibles, marking pens, pencils, masking tape, and fine-point marking pens.
- This is a "card" session that uses index cards in every step to generate interest and offer variety from the usual paper. Youth will need stacks of cards for Step 1, one card per person for Steps 2 and 5, three per person for Step 3, and six total cards for Step 4. Various sized cards are fine, as long as all cards for Step 1 are the same size.
- Consider bringing recipe cards instead of index cards for Step 2.

- Photocopy Handout 4. If you have more than 16 youth, you'll need more than one copy of Handout 4. Photocopy Handout 5 for each youth. Cut apart Handout 4.
- Bring paper and pencils if you choose to use the Bonus Option.

Invite Attention

Step 1: Make Lists of Great Length (10 minutes)

As youth enter, assign them to the *ear* group or *mouth* group and urge them to write, one per card, as many reasons as they can to explain why that body part is most critical to communication. Tell youth that each reason must begin with the letter the previous reason ended with, each must be written on a separate index card, and each must be taped end to end to form a long list. (Examples for ear: **Y**ou can't have talk without listenin**g**. … **G**ood communication requires hearing and understanding what the other say**s**. … **S**eeing with my eyes helps me listen bette**r**. … **R**epeating what the other says is a way to liste**n**. … **N**obody can communicate without listening.) Provide a stack of index cards, marking pens, and masking tape. Circulate to suggest that one youth write, while the others give ideas; one youth tears tape, while one youth tapes together the cards. Be sure that the cards are taped end to end. If you have more than 12 youth, form extra teams so no team is larger than six.

When most youth have arrived, have the teams hold up their lists and measure them against each other. Say something like, **Real lovers must go to great *lengths* to communicate with each other.** Ask, **Why is talking critical to communication?** Ask the mouth team to present a sampling of its list. Remind students that the mouth can listen by asking questions.

Ask, **Why is listening critical to communication?** Ask the ear team to present a sampling of its list. Remind students that the ears can encourage talking by the way they hear.

Ask, **Why is comparing not as helpful as working together to accomplish the common purpose of communication?** Have youth tape all lists end to end to show how far they can go with communication.

Dig into the Bible

Step 2:
Write a Recipe for Tasty Communication
(15–20 minutes)

Say, **Talking with someone of the opposite sex, especially someone you like, can be scary. Why?** Invite youth to answer honestly by receiving their answers with understanding. (Possible answers include: She might think what I say is stupid. I turn red. I get all tongue-tied. I don't know what to say. It's easy to talk to some guys but not the one I like. There's a lot riding on whether or not she likes what I say.) As youth respond, write each obstacle on an index card. Tape the cards to the wall and let youth choose one for which they want to find the solution. If two youth want the same obstacle, direct them to work independently to find the solution, recognizing that variety will help and two solutions are better than one. Emphasize that Ephesians 4 refers to the body of Christ and draws sharp contrast between living as part of that body and living a "worldly" life. The phrases to emphasize are "be made new in the attitude of your minds" and "put on the new self."

Give these instructions: **Search Ephesians 4:17–19, 25–32 for ingredients that would tackle the talk predicament you chose. Using at least three of these ingredients, write a recipe for tasty talk. Include ingredients, mixing instructions, and the dish that results.** Pass out index cards or recipe cards and write the five things to include on a chalkboard: (1) ingredients, (2) mixing instructions, (3) baking instructions, (4) the dish that results, and (5) the title of the recipe. Remind youth to include at least three ingredients from Ephesians 4:17–19, 25–32. (Dishes could include: Tasty Talk, Listening Lasagna, Communication Casserole.) Examples of ingredients and ways they might be mixed in include

- start with a generous dose of choosing to break the pattern of people who ignore God (v. 17);
- remove the pieces of futile thinking that may have fallen in when you cracked the ignoring patterns (v. 17);
- watch to be certain the mixture does not become hardened before adding the other ingredients because hardening of hearts will cause a dark result (v. 18);
- refuse the temptation to add more and more to the bowl because it will make the mixture unresponsive and indulgent (v. 19);
- add a cup of truthfulness and mix with the understanding that we are members of one body (v. 25);
- pour in anger, stirring it gently to keep it from gelling into sin (v. 26);

SESSION 3

Teacher Tip

Any time youth can give specific examples of what they have learned, you know they understand it. The recipes and comic strips help youth do this. Far from "busy work" these activities equip youth to give practical application to the principles they have studied in the Bible. Then when youth face real communication challenges, they'll have examples of how to apply biblical truth.

- guard your bowl from the greedy hands of the devil (v. 27);
- blend in a cup of honest work alternated with a cup of generous sharing (v. 28);
- stir in a quart of helpful and encouraging talk to add color and flavor to the dish (v. 29);
- put in a pinch of pleasing God's Spirit to connect with all above ingredients (v. 30);
- roll the mixture onto a floured surface and kneed out all lumps of bitterness, rage, anger, brawling, slander, and malice (v. 31);
- alternately stir in kindness and compassion to produce a rich and pliable batter (v. 32);

Final baking instructions could include
- keep the light on in the oven as the panful of mixture bakes into connection with God (v. 18);
- bake in a Please-the-Holy-Spirit oven for 15 minutes each morning (v. 30);
- refrigerate overnight in a redeemed refrigerator (v. 30);
- cool on a rack of kindness and compassion (v. 32).

Affirm youth generously as they write their recipes, reminding them to look in their Bibles for ideas. Ask volunteers to read their recipes. Highlight a wise ingredient or procedure in each. Discuss, **Why is talking much more than opening your mouth and listening much more than closing it? What ingredients make for good communication? How do we burn communication rather than produce a good result with it?**

Stress, **You make or break your relationships by the way you choose to communicate. Pick ingredients that help you talk, understand, solve problems, encourage, prompt, and more.** Invite youth to join you in a prayer committing yourselves to communicate lovingly. Explain that the next two steps will give us ideas for doing this.

Step 3: Create a Comic Strip (10 minutes)

Say, **Talking and listening are more than just conversation. They make all of life happier and easier to manage because communication equips you and your loved one to live life together. Let's give our group specific examples of this.** Give each youth one of the 16 topic cards cut from Handout 4. If you have more than 16 youth, let more than one talk on the same topic with different emphases. Urge youth, **Create a comic strip on how to talk and listen during this circumstance or in this place in a way that makes life happier or easier to manage.** Provide fine-point marking pens and index cards to use as the frames. Circulate as youth work, encouraging them to include specific words, a phrase from Ephesians 4:17–19, 25–32, and at least three frames. Remind youth that ideas, not artistic quality, are the primary goal of this activity.

As youth share their comic strips, highlight a specific way each comic strip shows how communication makes that area of a relationship happier or easier to manage.

Repeat, **Communication is more than what we do in our leisure time; it helps with problem solving, school, work, and much more.**

Live What You Learn

Step 4: Listen with Your Mouth and More (10 minutes)

Recall what the *ear* team said about using your ears to encourage talking and what the *mouth* team said about using questions to listen. Highlight, **We use every part of our body to encourage communication.** Ask,

- **How are mouths used to listen?** Write an **M** on an index card and tape it to the wall.
- **How are ears used to talk?** Write an **E** on an index card and tape it to the wall.
- **How is your head used to listen and speak?** Write an **H** on an index card and tape it to the wall.
- **How are eyes used to listen and speak?** Write an **E** on an index card and tape it to the wall.
- **How does a loving attitude help communication?** Write an **L** on an index card and tape it to the wall.
- **How is posture—the way you carry your body—used to listen and speak?** Write a **P** on an index card and tape it to the wall.
- **Can you give more examples of using the whole person to speak?**

Ask, **What did we spell with our six letters?** (ME HELP) Suggest that youth use the acronym ME HELP to remember all six talking and listening assets. Review that ME HELP stands for

> My **M**outh, **E**ars, **H**ead, **E**yes, **L**oving attitude, and **P**osture bring caring communication.

Give each youth a copy of Handout 5. Challenge them to find examples in the handout of how to use Mouths, Ears, Head, Eyes, Loving Attitude, and Posture to invite talk. To find these examples, youth must separate the

SESSION 3

Bonus Option

Invite youth to provide dating advice for one another. Have each youth write a question about communication. Shuffle the questions and redistribute them so everyone has a question to answer. Have the youth write their answers in advice-letter form. Have each youth read the question he or she received and the answer he or she wrote or redistribute the cards and letters again and read them aloud. Sample questions might include

- How do I get started talking to someone I like?
- How can I be honest without being too relaxed?
- How can I impress someone I like without being fake?
- How can I be myself and free the other person to be herself or himself?

block of letters into words. More than one idea can apply to each ME HELP aspect.

Call out M, then E, then H, and so on to invite youth to name the ideas they found. Remember that more than one idea can apply to each letter. Samples include the following: Say anything that starts with "I like the way you …" *(mouth)*. Ask questions with your mouth that invite your date to talk such as *(mouth, ears)*: "How did chemistry go this week?" "What's happening with the project you're working on at church?" "When do you feel afraid and what do you do about it?" "What do you remember about being a little kid?" "What do you daydream about?" "Who are your heroes?" "When do you feel most contented?" "Why are you a Christian?" Then listen with your ears, eyes, head, and posture. Open both ears to hear feelings as well as words *(ears)*. Look with your eyes to see what your friend feels and dreams *(eyes)*. Nod your head to encourage your friend to keep talking *(head)*. Let your attitude communicate that you really care what he or she thinks *(loving attitude)*. Eliminate attitudes of superiority or my-needs-are-more-important-than-your-needs *(loving attitude)*. After your ears hear, repeat back what you heard to make sure you understand *(ears, mouth)*. Let your head smile and show interest and project you-are-important *(head)*. Look right into the eyes of the one you're communicating with *(eyes)*. Lean your body toward the person to let your posture communicate interest *(posture)*. Reach out and touch the person to communicate that you're listening *(posture)*. Pose your body in a way that shows you're focused on what the person says *(posture)*. Say, "Tell me about it," and then listen with rapt attention *(mouth, ears, loving attitude)*.

Invite youth to name other examples for each letter from their own experience. Explain, **You have taken a garbled message and made it into something understandable. You can do the same thing with the barrage of garbled feelings that confront you every time you try to talk to someone you care about—one action at a time, like one little line to separate word from word, brings caring communication. You can create clear communication.**

Step 5:
Practice What You've Preached
(5–10 minutes)

Invite youth to practice communication with ME HELP actions: Seat youth in pairs with chairs facing each other. Direct one youth to tell the one across from her about the best and worst of that day, challenging both speaker and listener to use ME HELP. Change roles after two minutes, now challenging the new talker and listener to use ME HELP. Call for all to give feedback on what their partners did well and how they'd want to use that same skill in dating. Give each youth an index card and direct them to write ME HELP and its meaning. Suggest they mark Ephesians 4:17–19, 25–32 in their Bibles.

HANDOUT 4 — SESSION 3

School	Work
Family	Church
Problem solving	Free time
Dreams	Decision making
Time together	Time apart
Sickness	Bad mood
Disappointment	Triumph
Crisis	Pressure

SESSION 3— HANDOUT 5

Block of Talk Invitations

Find ways to use your **M**outh, **E**ars, **H**ead, **E**yes, **L**oving attitude, and **P**osture to invite talking. To find these, separate the block of letters into words and sentences.

SAYANYTHINGTHATSTARTSWITH"ILIKETHEWAYYOU…"ASKQUESTIONSWITHYOURMOUTHTHATINVITEYOURDATETOTALKSUCHAS:"HOWDIDCHEMISTRYGOTHISWEEK?""WHAT'SHAPPENINGWITHTHEPROJECTYOU'REWORKINGONATCHURCH?""WHENDOYOUFEELAFRAIDANDWHATDOYOUDOABOUTIT?""WHATDOYOUREMEMBERABOUTBEINGALITTLEKID?""WHATDOYOUDAYDREAMABOUT?""WHOAREYOURHEROES?""WHENDOYOUFEELMOSTCONTENTED?""WHEREAREALLTHEPLACESYOUHAVELIVEDANDWHATDIDYOULIKEABOUTEACH?""WHYAREYOUACHRISTIAN?"THENLISTENWITHYOUREARSEYESHEADANDPOSTUREOPENBOTHEARSTOHEARFEELINGSASWELLASWORDSLOOKWITHYOUREYESTOSEEWHATYOURFRIENDFEELSANDDREAMSNODYOURHEADTOENCOURAGEYOURFRIENDTOKEEPTALKINGLETYOURATTITUDECOMMUNICATETHATYOUREALLYCAREWHATHEORSHETHINKSELIMINATEATTITUDESOFSUPERIORITYORMYNEEDSAREMOREIMPORTANTTHANYOURNEEDSAFTERYOUREARSHEARREPEATBACKWHATYOUHEARDTOMAKESUREYOUUNDERSTANDLETYOURHEADSMILEANDSHOWINTERESTANDPROJECT"YOUAREIMPORTANT"LOOKRIGHTINTOTHEEYESOFTHEONEYOU'RECOMMUNICATINGWITHLEANYOURBODYTOWARDTHEPERSONTOLETYOURPOSTURECOMMUNICATEINTERESTREACHOUTANDTOUCHTHEPERSONTOCOMMUNICATETHATYOU'RELISTENINGPOSEYOURPOSTUREINAWAYTHATSHOWSYOU'REFOCUSEDONTHEPERSONSAY"TELLMEABOUTIT"ANDTHENLISTENWITHRAPTATTENTION

2 Corinthians 6:14–16; Galatians 5:22–23

SESSION 4

Is This the One?

Focus on a Goal Truth

Love depends much more heavily on choosing to consistently care than on finding a certain someone.

Understand Concerns Youth Have

- How can I tell if this is the one for me? Could I possibly be happy with two people?
- We're so much alike—but aren't I supposed to like someone opposite me?
- Is this difference really that important?

Connect Scripture to Youth Concerns

1. Examine the reasons similarity is a greater attraction than opposites.
2. Discover why Christianity is the first similarity, followed closely by values and dreams.
3. Pinpoint specific actions that help you choose someone like you to like you.

Gather Supplies and Prepare

- Bring extra Bibles, pencils, and index cards.
- Bring two inexpensive magnets for each youth (available in hardware stores).
- Bring paper and marking pens for Step 4.
- Photocopy one copy of Handout 6 for every six youth. Bring several pennies.

SESSION 4

Invite Attention

Step 1:
Find Why Opposites Won't Attract for Long
(10 minutes)

As youth enter give each a set of two magnets. Challenge them to make the magnets repel and attract by putting the poles together. For round magnets this is accomplished through turning one magnet over. Say, **In magnets, opposites attract. When people say "opposites attract" in dating, what do they mean?** After several youth comment, highlight, **Matching poles repel** (push apart) **and opposite poles attract** (stick together). **This works great with magnets. But it doesn't work so well in dating. Why not?** Use youth comments to explain that in dating, the fact that one is male and one is female is opposite enough.

Ask, **Why does similarity create closeness more naturally than opposites? How do opposites feed opposition?** Challenge youth to summarize the answers to these questions with four words, two words, and then one word. (Samples: Seek people like me; similarities attract; commonality. Or: You and I agree; together goals; we.) Urge youth, **Keep the set of magnets as a reminder that opposites attract applies to magnets, not to dating.**

Dig into the Bible

Step 2:
Discover Why the Best Couple Is a Good Trio
(10–15 minutes)

Transition to this next step by saying, **The main similarity that brings dating and marital happiness is that both people are Christians, not just people who go to church but people who honor God in their daily life. When people assume faith doesn't matter, they make huge mistakes. They compromise their dating and marital happiness. I'm going to make a mistake by changing a word or two in 2 Corinthians 6:14–16. Catch the mistake by watching in your Bible, then tell me the correction. I'll call on the first person who stands.** Read the first part of 2 Corinthians 6:14 with this mistake: **It's fine to be yoked together with unbelievers.**

The correct version is of course: "Do not be yoked together with unbelievers." Explain that to be yoked is to be united in close friendship or marriage and that a yoke connects two animals for work. We could say it connects people for work and play.

Ask for volunteers to make a mistake in the second sentence of verse 14, then the first and second questions of verse 15, the first question of verse 16, and the second sentence of verse 16. Finally, let youth make mistakes anywhere in 2 Corinthians 6:14–16, reading the whole passage while the group seeks to find the mistake(s).

Sample Mistakes

- For a righteous person can help a wicked one get better.
- Closeness can happen between light and darkness if they're both cute.
- Worshiping Christ or Belial (Satan) is no big deal, as long as you're sincere.
- If there's enough in common, it doesn't matter if you're a believer or not.
- Couples can work out disagreements between worship of God and worship of something else or worship of nothing else.
- God doesn't mind who we date or marry.
- Who I date is between me and my date; God has nothing to do with it.

Sample Corrections

- "For what do righteousness and wickedness have in common?"
- "Or what fellowship can light have with darkness?"
- "What harmony is there between Christ and Belial (Satan)?"
- "What does a believer have in common with an unbeliever?"
- "What agreement is there between the temple of God and idols?"
- "For we are the temple of the living God."
- As God has said: "I will live with them and walk among them, and I will be their God, and they will be My people."

Using the students' wise words, affirm them for seeing the difference between what couples tend to believe and what is really true. Say, **Now that you've had practice in finding mistakes, you'll be better at spotting them in dating and later in marriage.** Ask,

- **Why do people choose to think faith doesn't matter?** Guide youth to include the following: They see faith as a characteristic like blue eyes rather than the way it really is—a relationship that touches all of life. They start liking someone and make excuses for that person's lack of faith. They believe there are no cute or fun Christians. They haven't let their religion make a difference in their lives. They've had a bad experience with Christians.

SESSION 4

- **What mistake do people make when they refuse to value Christian commitment as a factor in choosing whom to date?** Help youth include these: They have less in common than two Christians. They have less fun because Christians are in touch with the Creator of fun. They have no one to help guide their relationship—Christians have God to help things go well between them. They assume Christianity doesn't impact everyday life and it does.
- **What mistake do people make when they refuse to value Christian commitment as a factor in choosing whom to marry?** Help youth include ideas like these: Two Christians tend to head the same direction because they seek to please God, but two who believe differently head different directions. A non-Christian may attend church to please the date but will quit after marriage so they do less together. The non-Christian tends to pull down the Christian. We need all the help we can get in living the Christian life. The more in common we have the better, and the ultimate commonality is active faith in Jesus Christ.
- **The best couple is a good trio: man, woman, and God. What phrase in 2 Corinthians 6:14–16 shows this?** ("I will live with them, … and they will be My people" in verse 16.) **What do you like about God helping your love life?**
- **Choose one of the questions in 2 Corinthians 5:14–16 to answer.**
- **To summarize, what do you think is the most important reason to date and marry a Christian according to 2 Corinthians 6:14–16?**

Step 3:
Determine What You Need besides Christianity
(10–15 minutes)

Stress, **Of course being a Christian alone is not enough to make a good dating relationship or a good marriage. Think privately about a Christian of the opposite sex that you know you wouldn't want to date or marry.** Don't allow youth to say anything about this person aloud, but watch for a moment as their faces show the feelings they have. Then say, **Don't mention your thoughts to anyone, but you now understand that Christian faith alone or the Christian label alone won't do it. We've got to see fruits that show this person is serious about God.**

Search Galatians 5:22–23 for other qualities you want in the one you marry. Instruct youth to raise their hands when they find one. Then say, **I'm coming around to see that you've each chosen a different quality. Get ready to tell me how you can express this quality in a**

SESSION 4

Christlike way. Check off in your Bible the ones youth choose. Samples of what they might say:

- A girl could show *love* by using her words to build up a boyfriend, not tear him down. A guy could show *love* by using his words to encourage, not ridicule girls.
- A guy could show *joy* by enjoying the simple things in life and not having to be the center of attention. A girl could show *joy* with security when tough times come.
- A girl could show *peace* by calmly managing a big test. A guy could show *peace* by competing fairly in sports and not attacking people just to win.
- A guy could show *patience* by listening with understanding. A girl could show *patience* by calmly persisting in responding to a difficult teacher.
- A girl could show *kindness* by speaking positively about her husband. A guy could show *kindness* by attacking the problem rather than attacking his wife.
- A guy could show *goodness* by telling the truth. A girl could show *goodness* by doing the right thing even when it's tough.
- A girl could show *faithfulness* by seeing her husband as a person, not a vehicle to money and security. A guy could show *faithfulness* by seeing his wife as a person, not a provider of household services or a possession he can boss around.
- A guy could be *gentle* by talking to kids, by valuing each person he talks to, and by never forcing himself on a girl. A girl could be *gentle* by smiling across the room.
- A guy could show *self-control* by talking through his temper rather than hitting his girlfriend/wife. A girl could show *self-control* by translating whining and critical words into cooperative and caring words.

Obviously both guys and girls could express the fruit of the Spirit in all these ways. Guide youth to bring this out by asking, **Why do we think some characteristics in this passage are for women only? men only? Why are Christlike characteristics for everyone?**

Review, **Opposites attract applies to magnets, not to people. The fact that you are male and female is opposite enough and adds the variety you need. Look for similar values and similar dreams.** Ask, **Why are values and dreams so important in a solid love relationship?** Highlight Christianity as the first similarity, followed closely by values and dreams. What else is important in love? (humor, fun, positive attitude, work, more)

SESSION 4

Bonus Option

"Is there just one?" Guide youth to discuss this question by sending half the youth to one side of the room and half the youth to the other side.

Assign one side to support *Yes, there's only one person for each person. Only our soulmate will make us happy.*

Assign the other side to support *No, there are many people with whom each person could be happy. We find someone with whom we have a lot in common and build a life together.*

Before speaking, each side must tell the other one reason the other side might be right.

Conclude the discussion by saying, **Marriage is a creation between two people who choose to commit to each other. It's unlikely there's only one person you could be happy with. To be happy, choose the person with whom you have much in common.**

Step 4: Choose Someone like You to Like You (10 minutes)

Ask, **So how do you find this perfect trio member, one who loves God and loves you? It's not easy but three things help: (1) Realize the story's not over yet; (2) Date only people you would marry; and (3) Free yourself from the find-that-perfect-someone wait so you can go ahead and enjoy life now.** Invite youth to share how they have done these. Samples include the following:

1. **Realize the story's not over yet.** I remember that today's circumstances don't doom me to a life of loneliness. It takes time to build good relationships—reading a love story makes it sound easy but in real life it takes hours, days, or years to get to the bottom of the page.
2. **Date only people you would marry.** I don't talk about marriage on the first date, but I do notice character traits and refuse "we're just dating so it doesn't matter." I look for someone who is already a strong Christian rather than try to make him or her over into my image. I recognize that I could fall in love before I realize it. I don't want to start dating someone I'd break up with.
3. **Free yourself from the find-that-perfect-someone wait so you can go ahead and enjoy life now.** Finding someone won't make me happy. I have to be happy first. There's more than one person with whom I can be happy. Romance is not a magical happily-ever-after as much as it is a creation between two committed people.

Live What You Learn

Step 5: Decide to Build Lasting Love (10 minutes)

Guide youth to apply the tips they composed in Step 4 and the Scripture truths they discovered in Steps 2 and 3 to real-life problems. Distribute cards to each youth and invite them to write a letter asking advice on a problem related to "Is this the one?"

Display the cards upside down in the space provided on Handout 6. If you have more than six youth, give each half-dozen youth their own handout pie, dividing the cards evenly among the pies. Direct youth, **Drop a penny on the handout and give at least two sentences of advice based on the pie piece the penny falls closest to.** Youth can use one sentence from the response written in that piece but must add the other sentence, drawing on discoveries. For the blank pie piece, they choose a question from the pile and give both sentences. Encourage scriptural, specific, and true-to-life advice.

Agree, **Even though we say with our words that it's good to date and marry a caring Christian with whom we have much in common, we fall short in real life. What action or attitude will you express to show your commitment to find a person with whom you can build a lifelong love?** Ask each youth around the circle to name something different. (Samples: Be patient. Only date someone I'd marry. Take seriously warnings by family and friends that there may be a problem. Never go out with someone before I know them at least a little. Talk with God before and during every date. Be honest with myself about similarities and differences.) Assure youth that God will help them find someone with whom they have much in common and will help them be content both before marriage, during marriage, and all their lives if they choose not to marry.

SESSION 4

Teacher Tip

When giving advice in a church setting, youth tend to give standard church answers such as "Pray" and "Trust God." Certainly these answers are true, but youth need to know *how* to live them before these true answers can do any good. So when youth give a standard answer, prod them to specify with "What sentence will you say when you pray?" or "What action will show that you do trust God?" or "How will people know you're doing that by watching you?"

SESSION 4 — HANDOUT 6

Problem Pie

Choose one slice and discover God's advice based on these starter responses and the Bible passages you've been studying in this session. **Think:** What actions while I date would keep me from having to eat this piece of problem pie after I marry?

Problem: He'll get better after we marry.

Response: This is a *huge* myth. If anything, he'll get harder to live with. We tend to put on our best face while dating. Then after marriage, we tend to show more of our weaknesses. Know your love's weaknesses before you commit to each other because you'll see them in magnified form after marriage.

Problem: I know he really believes—he just doesn't like to talk about it.

Response: If he doesn't talk about God, God is likely not very important to him. Too often we make excuses for people's lack of faith. Date only people who already demonstrate commitment to God in their character, words, time choices, and activity choices.

Problem: I can help her become a Christian.

Response: Evangelistic dating seldom works. In fact it usually works in reverse—the non-Christian tends to pull the dedicated Christian away from God because the Christian will compromise in the name of tolerance and love. Then the Christian finds himself or herself ignoring God, even participating in wrong behaviors. Date only people who are already Christians.

Problem: We can handle the differences in beliefs; we'll just let our kids choose when they grow up.

Response: If you can handle the differences to your beliefs, neither of you is very committed to your beliefs. Faith should be a passion that encompasses all of life. Watering it down compromises both you and the one you love. And kids tend to believe what they see in real life. Faith isn't something children can choose like clothing at the mall. It is the working of the Holy Spirit within you to sanctify you that you might have the blessings of redemption and lead a godly life. (See 1 Corinthians 2:14 and 6:11.)

Problem: Opposites attract. Of course we're very different, but it's supposed to be that way.

Response: Being male and female is opposite enough. The more alike you are in temperament, values, dreams, goals, and passions the better love relationship you can build.

Colossians 3:12–17

SESSION 5

Is It Love or Friendship?

Focus on a Goal Truth

The best dates and marriages are both/and, not either/or. They have the best of both friendship and love.

Understand Concerns Youth Have

- How can I tell if it's love or friendship?
- I can't date him. It would mess up our friendship.
- There's nothing you can really do; romance either happens or it doesn't.

Connect Scripture to Youth Concerns

1. Examine what we want in a spouse and how we can be what someone seeks.
2. Discover friendship actions and how to live them in five settings.
3. Pinpoint ways to be a friend in real-life problems.

Gather Supplies and Prepare

- Bring extra Bibles, pencils, paper, marking pens, and clear tape.
- Photocopy two copies of Handout 7 for each youth.
- Bring a ballpoint pen for each youth.
- For every two to six youth, photocopy one copy of Handout 8; cut and assemble with clear tape.
- Bring extra paper and pencils if you choose to do the Bonus Option.

SESSION 5

Teacher Tip

Two reactions to head off at the pass during this activity are

1. **"We're too old for paper dolls."** Agree that yes, they are too old for paper dolls, but they are now mature enough to use a tool to discover Bible truths. With a positive attitude, point out that wise people know that a tool or prop helps us focus on what we're learning and helps us remember it. Say, **As you create this paper image God can help you picture and work toward a happy marriage. And you'll remember your dreams because you pictured them.**

2. **"She'll have a great body."** Discourage focus on the physical by stating that true beauty is more than skin deep, that looks tell little about how fun that person is to be with or how easy that person will be to live with. Agree that God does make men and women attractive. Then thank God for the way He made us.

Invite Attention

Step 1: Custom-Make Your Mate (10–15 minutes)

As youth enter, say, **We all have dreams about who we want to marry and what he or she will be like.** Challenge youth to put these dreams on paper by creating a custom-made mate using Handout 7. Provide clear tape to assemble the custom people. Rather than try to collect enough scissors for everyone, allow youth to tear their pieces.

Ask each youth to point out on the paper doll one characteristic they really want in the one they marry, assuring them that you know they want more than this one. Ask, **Why is this quality important to you? How will it make a good marriage?** Urge each youth to pick something different. Say, **We'd all like to make the perfect mate. What's wrong and right about this?** Using youth's comments, stress such truths as the following: A dream could keep us from recognizing the right one when he or she comes along, but it's more likely to help us recognize certain values. It's wrong to expect someone to be perfect, but thinking ahead about what we need keeps us from focusing on looks or status or other shallow measures of humanity. It's dangerous to try to make a person in our image instead of God's, but it is good to recognize God's good work in people as well as people who avoid God's good.

Say, **No matter how much we'd like to create a perfect mate, the one mate we can control is ourselves. Repeat the custom-made mate process for *yourself*. What kind of mate does God want you to be? How can you be like what you want someone else to be? How does God want you to prepare right now for marriage?** Give youth a new Handout 7. As youth work, circulate and suggest quietly, **We tore the pieces before and we'll tear them this time. What rough edges does God want to smooth over in your actions, attitudes, and words?** As youth finish, invite each to name the quality they think God most wants them to grow right now. Stress, **We're all growing toward the person God wants us to be, and as we make deliberate choices to care, we become great mates. One of the best mate qualities is friendship.** Invite all to pray privately for God's guidance in becoming a great mate.

Dig into the Bible

Step 2:
Decide to Be a Friend
(10–15 minutes)

Transition to the next step by saying, **Friendship helps us both work on ourselves and bring out good qualities in others. How has a friend helped you become a better person?** As youth volunteer, urge them to cite friendship actions of the opposite sex, but welcome examples from any friendship that has helped them. Ask, **Based on your experience, why is friendship the strongest base for any romance?**

Using youth's comments explain that the best way to learn to be a good friend is to remember that they share in the mind of Christ. (See Colossians 3:1–4.) Recall that they have briefly glanced at Colossians 3:12–17 while doing the Create-a-Mate Handout but will now delve more deeply. Give each youth a ballpoint pen, direct them to hold up their left hands, and guide them to write on the tip of each finger of their left hand these areas of life:

- Thumb: *home*
- Index finger: *school*
- Middle finger: *work/chores*
- Ring finger: *church*
- Pinky: *fun*

Then divide the phrases of Colossians 3:12–16 among youth and direct them to tell the group how to show friendship with their appointed Colossians 3 phrase in all five places. Feel free to photocopy and give as idea starters these sample phrases:

Therefore, as God's chosen people, holy and dearly loved—At **school** I'll treat every person as a unique and valuable creation of God because I'm one too. At **home** …

Clothe yourselves with compassion—At **home** I'll feel the feelings of my parent or sibling before reacting since compassion means to feel (passion) with (com). This will teach me how to relate to a spouse one day. During **fun** …

Clothe yourselves with … kindness—During **fun** with friends the way I say things is as important as what I say. So I'll avoid mean sarcasm and putdowns. At **church** …

Clothe yourselves with … humility—I'll be teachable at **work,** realizing this prompts friendship between my boss and me. At **school** …

SESSION 5

Clothe yourselves with … gentleness—At **church** I'll show interest in everyone, even those several years younger or older than I am. This makes friendship, not cliques. During **chores** …

Clothe yourselves with … patience—At **school** I'll gain patience to handle the rough teacher by talking with my friend _____. During **chores** …

Bear with each other—During **fun** with my friend I'll sometimes do what she wants to do rather than what I want to do. At **church** …

Forgive whatever grievances you may have against one another. Forgive as the Lord forgave you—People make mistakes. So I'll forgive my co-worker at **work** rather than hold a grudge and spread a rumor. At **church** …

And over all these virtues put on love, which binds them all together in perfect unity—When my sister and I disagree at **home**, we'll find some way to understand each other. At **school** …

Let the peace of Christ rule in your hearts—If I feel like I have more than my fair share of **chores** at home, I'll talk in a peaceful way. That will help us work things out. At **church** …

And be thankful—When I'm talking to my friend _____ at **school**, I'll be certain to share what's going well instead of just complain about the problems. At **home** …

Let the word of Christ dwell in you richly as you teach and admonish one another—At **home** we'll gently point out each other's weaknesses so we can grow more loving. During **fun** …

Sing psalms, and hymns and spiritual songs with gratitude in your hearts to God—During **fun** my friend and I will try listening to Christian music rather than regular stuff. At **home** …

Remind youth that as it says in Colossians 3:17, whatever they do can bring good for God, and if they are bringing good for God, they will be building strong friendships. Recite together Colossians 3:17, each youth putting in his or her own first name in place of "you." For example: "And whatever *Megan does*, whether in word or deed … through Him."

As time allows, invite youth to share other verses in the Bible that teach them how to be friends. Discuss Colossians 3:12–17 and other verses with

- **How are both friendship and romance a part of marriage?**
- **What would be the differences between friendship with the opposite sex and love? What would be the extra ingredient or ingredients?**
- **What's empty about a romantic relationship without friendship?**

Step 3:
Use Words to Show Friendship
(10 minutes)

Repeat that good romance always includes an element of friendship. Emphasize, **One of the best friendship skills is affirmation. Through it you show that you believe people are God's chosen, holy, and loved creation** (Colossians 3:12). **Use your words to make your spouse feel better about life, not worse. Let's practice affirmation with each other. Pretend you are speaking to your spouse. Half the room gives a feel-worse complaint; the other side changes it to affirmation.** Start by offering feel-worse statements like these samples to which youth can give affirmations:

Feel-Worse Statements

"Ewwww, you're so sweaty and stinky!"

"You are always late!"

"Why won't you spend time with me?"

"Don't you ever stop studying?"

"I can't see in this steamy bathroom."

Affirmations

"You must have had a great workout. What did you enjoy about it?"

"I feel loved and respected when you're on time."

"How was your time with your friends?"

"Why don't we study together? I could help you with math, and you could help me with English."

"I love the way a bathroom smells after a shower."

Step 4:
Roll-a-Problem
(10 minutes)

Agree, **It's easier to talk about than to live biblical friendship characteristics such as affirmation, compassion, kindness, humility, gentleness, patience, bearing with, forgiveness, love, unity, peace, thankfulness, teaching, admonishing, and singing. This is especially true when there's a problem or when one person's in a bad mood. But we can be a friend by deliberately choosing to do so. God will give us the power. Let's practice with this problem cube.** Display Handout 8, which you have photocopied, cut, and folded into a cube. Choose a youth to roll it. Direct this youth to name a romantic action and a friendship action that would help solve this real-life problem. Remind all youth that

SESSION 5

Bonus Option

As time allows, let youth make a wish list of what they want in a spouse, drawing on Colossians 3:12–17 for ideas. Then guide youth to recognize that, because they are real, they are wish-granters in an even better way than a fairy godmother or Santa Claus. Direct them to write next to five items on their list how they could grant this wish. Samples:

- I want someone understanding.
- I want someone cute.
- I want someone forever.
- I could listen well and tell why I understand.
- I could let my personality make me attractive.
- I'll attack the problem rather than the person so we can solve our problems and stay together forever.

Invite youth to talk with God about the wishes He wants them to grant both now and in the future.

as it says in Colossians 3:17, whatever they do can bring good for God, and if they are bringing good for God, they will be building strong friendships. Repeat the game until every youth has a turn to roll and name a specific friendship and romantic action. If the same problem comes up more than once, the youth should name different romantic and friendship actions to show that there are many ways to approach each predicament and that more than one action can be used each time. Or, they can name a new problem. Discuss with

- **Why do we tend to believe these things won't happen to us?**
- **How similar are friendship and romantic actions?**
- **How does friendship keep romance going?**

Repeat that the essence of friendship is saying words and doing actions that please God and show love for people and that this is especially important during hard times. Recite Colossians 3:17 together again, each youth putting in his or her own first name in place of "you."

Live What You Learn

Step 5: Let Friendship Be Your Motto (10 minutes)

Stress, **So the answer is both/and. Friendship *and* romance are both critical to marital happiness, but you need a heavier dose of friendship.** Call for youth to share other tips from God for growing friendship in romantic relationships and later in marriage. Then guide foursomes to create a motto that summarizes the advice God recommends. Let the motto include at least three truths and spell a word. Provide paper. Sample motto:

Love includes T.R.U.E. friendship if it

- **T**akes time to listen to each other's joys and sorrows.
- **R**ecognizes the label "Christian" is not as important as choosing to do daily kindness in Christ's name.
- **U**nderscores enjoying the simple stuff of life together.
- **E**xists to bring happiness to the family unit and spill that happiness into the world.

Repeat together Colossians 3:17, guiding youth to read from their own Bibles. Choose one translation and share so all can read in unison. Thank God for friendship and the opportunity to grow it.

HANDOUT 7 — SESSION 5

Custom-Make Your Mate

Tear out this paper doll and then attach clothes and features to picture the kind of person you want to marry. If you don't see the feature you want, tear it from the blank sections on this page and label it. Focus on personality characteristics rather than looks.

An outgoing heart.

Thinks well and uses brain to make wise choices.

Eyes that see what to do and when.

Eyes that look me in the eye.

Brain that _____.

Eyes that _____.

Eyes that see the good in people.

Ears that hear my hopes and dreams.

Ears that care about simple daily stuff.

Ears that listen to joy and pain around them.

Ears that _____.

Clothed with _____ and _____ (choose from Colossians 3:12–14).

Clothed with _____ and _____ (choose from Colossians 3:15–17).

A quiet heart.

Feet that _____.

A heart that _____.

47

SESSION 5— HANDOUT 8

Role-a-Problem

Roll this cube and guide youth to name a romantic action and a friendship action that would help solve it. If the same problem comes up more than once, the youth should name different romantic and friendship actions to show that there are many ways to approach each predicament and that more than one action can be used each time:

Face 1 — What friendship action and romantic action will help with this situation? You're sick with the stomach flu, look a little green, and vomit all night.

Face 2 — What friendship action and romantic action will help with this situation? You both want to go to your parents' home on Christmas Day; they live two days' drive apart.

Face 3 — What friendship action and romantic action will help with this situation? You don't have enough money to pay this month's bills.

Face 4 — What friendship action and romantic action will help with this situation? He or she complains about the surprise you spent all day planning.

Face 5 — What friendship action and romantic action will help with this situation? The baby is crying at 3:00 A.M. and your spouse won't take a turn rocking her.

Face 6 — What friendship action and romantic action will help with this situation? You wreck his or her new car.

Genesis 39:1–23, 41:1, 9–13, 45; Philippians 4:8

SESSION 6

Is It Okay to Flirt?

Focus on a Goal Truth

There's nothing wrong with letting someone know you're interested in him or her. There's much wrong with attracting someone for impure reasons.

Understand Concerns Youth Have

- If it's meant to be, won't it just happen?
- I don't know how to flirt.
- I don't want to be like those people at school who flirt—you can tell they're fake.

Connect Scripture to Youth Concerns

1. Examine the difference between letting someone know you care and wrong flirting.
2. Discover Bible adjectives that describe good flirting.
3. Determine ways to avoid connections that hurt and make connections that count.

Gather Supplies and Prepare

- Bring extra Bibles, pencils, and paper.
- Bring a paper lunch sack. Photocopy Handout 9. Put a few sheets of blank paper behind it. Cut on the dotted lines. Discard the title. Fold and put inside the bag the strips from Handout 9. Keep the strips from the blank paper to give to youth for Step 1.
- Bring a tape or CD of contemporary Christian music and something to play it on.

- Wrap a ball of yarn large enough to be unwrapped across a circle of your youth as many times as there are youth. Bring scissors.
- Photocopy the case studies in Step 5. Make extra copies if you have more than 16 youth; give one case to every four youth.
- Invite couples with stories to tell if you decide to do the Bonus Option.

Invite Attention

Step 1: Bag Bad Flirting (10 minutes)

As youth enter, invite them to join the circle of chairs you have set up. Distribute blank strips of paper the size of those on Handout 9 and direct youth to write on the paper a way to let someone of the opposite sex know you like him or her. When it is time to start, gather the strips in a paper lunch sack that already contains folded strips from Handout 9. Blow up the sack, twist the top, and explain that youth will play "hot bag," an adaptation of hot potato. Guide youth to practice passing the sack around the circle lightly like a balloon, passing it only to their left, not holding it, and not throwing it across the circle. Explain, **Pass the bag while the music plays. When the music stops, the person holding the bag opens it, pulls out an action, and tells what would make this good flirting and what would make this bad flirting. For this session, we'll define flirting as letting someone of the opposite sex know that you're interested in dating him or her.** To keep it fair, don't watch where the bag is to stop the music. Instead appoint a youth to stand with you and watch to see who has the bag when the music stops. If you don't have music to play, hum "Jesus Loves Me, This I Know" and stop at different points of it during each round. Turn and listen as youth draw out a slip. Sample answers youth might give include

- *Look right into the person's eyes.* This would be good flirting when it's sincere. It would be bad if you're attracting the person to get something or to make someone else jealous.
- *Smile when the person looks at you.* This would be good flirting if you are genuinely interested. It would be bad if something terrible has just happened because it would look like you're laughing at the person.
- *Be there when the person comes around the corner.* This would be good if it's occasional. It would be bad if you're chasing the person—you can know this if you're doing all the "being there" and the other person doesn't give much effort.

SESSION 6

Affirm youth's wise distinctions, hearing at least one distinction for every slip in the bag. Say, **Let's look in the Bible to see how close we came to describing good flirting. Remember that flirting is letting someone know you care. God is interested in your romances and shows you how to relate in ways that work.**

Dig into the Bible

Step 2: Embrace Good Flirting (10 minutes)

Challenge youth, **Let this Bible verse be your motto for flirting. Underline in your Bible the adjectives** (describing words) **as one of you reads Philippians 4:8 aloud.** Invite a youth to read Philippians 4:8 from his or her Bible while the others follow along and underline adjectives in theirs. Ask, **Which quality would you most appreciate in someone flirting with you?** (Samples: I want to know his motives are **pure** and not designed to get something from me. I want to know she's **true** in her flirting, that she wants to know me. If he's using eye contact and waiting for me, that makes me feel **excellent.**) After several or all have chosen a word, invite volunteers to name all the adjectives that describe good flirting according to Philippians 4:8 (true, noble, right, pure, lovely, admirable, excellent, praiseworthy). Congratulate youth on their memory and cite that they remembered because they've heard others use these words. As we hear and live the Bible, we'll remember how to live for God. Ask, **What do you like about these adjectives for living? Why do they make for good dating as well as flirting?** Thank God for giving such good advice.

Step 3: Gather Evidence that He or She Is Good for You (10–15 minutes)

Transition to the next Bible passage with *Who* **you flirt with is as important as** *how* **you flirt. What mistakes do we make in the who department?** (Samples: Choose someone by looks alone. Flirt with people before we know anything about their character. Flirt with everyone rather than a special one. Choose someone who is sweet but isn't a Christian. Choose someone who is a Christian but doesn't walk the talk. Flirt with a friend's boyfriend or girlfriend. Give in to someone's games.)

Emphasize, **Problems with attraction are not new. People in the Bible made wise and foolish choices. The wise choices helped, the foolish choices hurt. We'll read about a fellow named Joseph who**

Teacher Tip

A simple prop like a bag with questions in it encourages youth to talk more freely about close-to-heart subjects such as how to let someone know you care. Give each youth a turn with the bag by introducing a rule that once you answer a question, you pass the bag to your right (or left). Also let only the person holding the bag do any talking. This equalizes talking and listening.

SESSION 6

made good choices in the midst of bad. Guide youth to turn to Genesis 39:1–23 and to mark in the margin of their Bibles the feelings Joseph had at each juncture. Invite one youth to read aloud, pausing where you cue him or her, while the others mark. If youth prefer not to write in their Bibles, guide them to slip paper under the Bible page and write on the place where the paper sticks out. Sample verses and feelings:

- **39:1–2**—feeling rich, lucky, secure
- **39:3–5**—feeling blessed, powerful, confident
- **39:6–7**—feeling attractive, flattered, then certain this is not right
- **39:8**—feeling if I just explain she'll understand, feeling nervous
- **39:9–10**—feeling hounded and tempted, wondering if he should give in
- **39:11–12**—feeling trapped, feeling certain of an escape from the temptation, feeling like running
- **39:13–20**—feeling falsely accused, betrayed, ugly, scared
- **39:21–23**—feeling like God is still helping me, feeling like life might go on

Apply to life what youth discovered in the Bible with

- **Since Joseph got thrown in prison, does that mean he did the wrong thing?** (Not at all. Sometimes it takes a long time before we see the good of our choices. An immediate "bad" result like being broken up with can lead to very good results like meeting someone even more wonderful.)
- **How long did Joseph have to stay in prison before he saw any good result according to chapters 40 and 41?** (We aren't sure, but we know it was "some time later" that he interpreted the cupbearer's and baker's dreams [40:1]. It was two years before he interpreted Pharaoh's dream [41:1]. It was later when he married [41:45].)
- **God helped Joseph do good even after he was in prison. He became a leader in 39:21–23. He told the truth to a cupbearer and a baker in chapter 40. The cupbearer forgot Joseph for awhile but later helped him (40:23; 41:9–13). Why is following Christ's leading, even in awful circumstances, worth it?** (God guides us and we know we can trust Him. It makes bad situations more bearable. It wins friends in the long run.)
- **Joseph passed up a woman who was not good for him. Later he married. Why is picking the right person worth the wait?** (Samples: We'll spend a lifetime together so a few years is worth that. Hurry may doom me to a lifetime of sadness.)

Stress, **Sometimes it seems like forever before we find someone we like who likes us back. This is more a problem with our society than something God put on you. In our society we marry as much as 10** years after we feel like being matched because we have a long period of education. Know that it's a tough circumstance but God will help you through. **What tips can you share for ways God is already helping you?** (Samples: Make connections with people who might help you later like Joseph did with the cupbearer, not because they might help you but because it's the right thing to do. Do the right thing because people do notice. Do the right thing because it builds trust.) After several youth share, thank God for His ever-present help.

Step 4:
Name Your Connections
(10–15 minutes)

Repeat, **Our connections to present people help us find and grow relationships with other people, one of which might become a marriage. Let's tell each other in this group what we appreciate about our friendships.** Explain that you will toss a ball of yarn across the room as you tell the person to whom you throw it what you appreciate. For example, "I'll throw to Dierdre to say her cheerful greetings at church always make me feel confident. She gives me courage to risk talking to the guy I like." When Dierdre receives the yarn, have her wrap it around her wrist, then choose and thank someone else, tossing the yarn to him or her. Continue until everyone catches, wraps, and passes the yarn. The leader should be the last receiver.

Point out the web of connections in the middle. Say, **This web shows but a few of the connections we enjoy in our group. A relationship with someone of the opposite sex is similar to this. Flirting is the first connection, talking casually becomes the next, and so on until two people build enough connections that they want to stay in close contact for life. It's called marriage. Remembering Philippians 4:8, what other connections might God want you to make in this group as friends?** (Samples: Speak to everyone rather than just my close friends. Notice and share sadness. Notice and share joys.) After several ideas ask, **Again remembering Philippians 4:8, what do you most look forward to about connecting with someone you may marry?** (Samples: Someone I can share everyday events with, a friend who will live with me.) Use youth's words to show that good connections between people are treasured gifts from God.

Guide youth to gently tug on the web. Ask, **How do our connections affect one another?** (Sample: When one hurts, we feel the tug. When one is happy, we rejoice with him or her.) Use scissors to cut the web at youth's wrists, and direct them to help each other tie the yarn around their wrists as a symbol of their connection to one another and as hope for connection

SESSION 6

with someone they might marry. Stress, **Who you choose to connect with matters. How you choose to connect matters. Keep in touch with people, care for those you come in contact with, love people for God's sake.** Reread Philippians 4:8.

Live What You Learn

Step 5: Set Up Ways to Cross Each Other's Paths (10 minutes)

Invite a youth to present this dialog with you or another youth, one reading the dark print and one the light print:

Flirting, or attracting another's initial attention, is just the first step to establishing a strong relationship. Each member of the couple must continue to make connections after that to build a relationship that will last.

But if it's meant to be, won't it just happen?

No. We're not puppets on a string that God manipulates to suit His purposes. Instead we work hand-in-hand with Him to bring His good relationships.

But can't God bring two people who can love each other together?

Certainly. But those two have to make decisions and take action to start a relationship and keep it going.

You mean if one person doesn't do anything, a good relationship could never start or could fall apart?

Yes, you could miss someone with whom you'd be very happy; but you can build happiness with someone else. Let's talk about ways to make connections so that rather than mourn what didn't happen, we can discover what can happen.

What are ways besides flirting to set up connections? (Invite all youth to answer this.) **And what do we do about the barriers that come up when we try to connect?**

SESSION 6

Photocopy and distribute these case studies and invite teams to answer with an action, an attitude, a sentence, and a communication (phone call; e-mail; letter; etc.) that will help:

I've been friendly, I look at him at all the right times and drop hints. But he still doesn't ask me out. Is it meant to be or not?
An action that might help is
An attitude that might help is
A sentence that might help is
A communication that might help is

What's wrong with me? I'm reasonably intelligent, care about God, and treat people right. I hope I'm attractive and interesting to be around. Why am I not dating and other people are?
An action that might help is
An attitude that might help is
A sentence that might help is
A communication that might help is

I plan to look her right in the eye and say something friendly, but I freeze up when she comes around the corner. Why can I talk to any girl but her?
An action that might help is
An attitude that might help is
A sentence that might help is
A communication that might help is

Sometimes when I'm friendly, people take it the wrong way. They think I like them romantically, but I'm just treating them well, like I would any person. How can I keep from being misunderstood without hurting people's feelings?
An action that might help is
An attitude that might help is
A sentence that might help is
A communication that might help is

Close with something like **The timing of connecting with someone you care about can be tricky, but when two people listen to God and work with Him, they can build something beautiful.** Pray together for the ability to be true, noble, right, pure, lovely, admirable, excellent, and praiseworthy (Philippians 4:8).

Bonus Option

Invite happily married couples of all ages to tell the group how they met, how they let the other know they were interested in dating, and a time one misunderstood the other's message and how they managed it. Encourage each couple to speak for five minutes maximum, and then invite students' questions. The goal of this panel discussion is to show that all couples agonize at least to some degree in meeting and getting to know each other, but the good results are worth passing through the agony.

SESSION 6 — HANDOUT 9

Good Flirt Actions/Bad Flirt Actions

Wink or bat your eyes.

Look right into the person's eyes.

Smile when the person looks at you.

Be there when the person comes around the corner.

WALK TOGETHER.

SIT TOGETHER.

Write a letter even if you live in the same town.

SAVE A SEAT FOR THE PERSON OR WAIT FOR THE PERSON TO ARRIVE BEFORE JOINING THE OTHERS.

Make a point to speak each time you see that person.

Tell about things that are important to you and to that person.

SAY HI WITH INTEREST IF THIS PERSON HAPPENS TO CALL.

Look at this person a lot.

Draw this person in with your eyes.

Matthew 6:19–21, 25–34

SESSION 7

What if He Doesn't Like Me?

Focus on a Goal Truth

Worry is one of the main things we do in dating and waiting to date. Turn your worries into conversation with God to figure out what to do about each worry.

Understand Concerns Youth Have

- What if he doesn't like me?
- I don't know what to say to her.
- Have I done enough to let him know I'm interested or should I do more?

Connect Scripture to Youth Concerns

1. Examine when to worry and when not to worry.
2. Discover how to turn worries into solutions.
3. Help each other with specific worry problems such as looks, courage, and self-pity.

Gather Supplies and Prepare

- Bring extra Bibles, paper, pencils, and fine-tipped marking pens in a variety of colors.
- Photocopy Handouts 10 and 11 for each person. Cut out the pieces of Handout 11 and place each in a separate business-size envelope.
- Bring rocks, fine-tipped paint brushes, paint, and newspapers if you choose the Bonus Option.
- Bring index cards.

SESSION 7

- Write on the chalkboard: "Worry is good when _____, but worry is bad when _____."

Invite Attention

Step 1: Correct the Mistakes (10 minutes)

As youth enter, pair them, giving each pair a copy of Handout 10, and challenge them to find and correct the mistakes in this retelling of Matthew 6:19–21, 25–34. Say, **Work with a partner. One of you read the Bible passage aloud from the New International Version of the Bible while the other finds and corrects the mistakes on this sheet**. This activity guides youth to learn the facts of the passage so they can study it in the next steps. (In the passage below, the mistakes are italicized and the corrections are in parentheses.)

Store (Do not store) up for yourselves treasures on earth, *keeping them safe in a box* (where moth and rust destroy), and where thieves *can't get them* (break in and steal). But store up for yourselves treasures in *the bank* (heaven), where moth and rust do not destroy, and where *only some thieves* (thieves do not) break in and steal. For where your treasure is, there *you will be rich* (your heart will be also). … Therefore I tell you, *worry* (do not worry) about your life, what you will *say or do* (eat or drink); or about your body, what you will wear. Is not *food* (life) more important than *life* (food), and *clothes* (the body) more important than *the body* (clothes)? Look at the birds of the air; they do not sow or reap or store away in barns, and yet your heavenly Father feeds them. Are you not much *less* (more) valuable than they? Who of you by worrying can add a single hour to his life? And why do you worry about *status* (clothes)? See how the lilies of the field grow. They do not labor or spin. Yet I tell you that not even Solomon in all his splendor was dressed like one of these. If that is how God clothes the grass of the field, which is *gorgeous to look at* (here today and tomorrow is thrown into the fire), will He not much more clothe you, O you of little faith? So do not worry, saying, 'What shall we eat?' or 'What shall we drink?' or 'What shall we wear?' For the *holy* (pagans) run after all these things, and your heavenly Father *fusses at them for it* (knows that you need them). But seek *last* (first) His kingdom and His *riches* (righteousness), and all these things will be *withheld from you* (given to you) as well. Therefore do not worry about tomorrow, for tomorrow will worry about itself. Each day has enough trouble of its own.

Manufacturers Coupons needed
COFFEE - TEA - CHOC.
Cereals
Macaroni products & TOMATO SAUCES, ETC
Salad dressing - VINEGAR - pickles
Soups
Personal hygiene products - Toothpaste, RAZOR, ETC
Juices
Crackers - COOKIES
Vegetables
Fruits
Jellies & jams
Peanut butter - CANDY, ETC.
Kleenx & paper products
Cleaning products
Jello & Puddings
Spices

fe is that worry
tain things is
t are already
t to do about the
l about it and
their heads and
en for His

o the tune of a
a song, a com-
rt the tune or
the format.
Then invite vol-
unteers to recite the verse. Point out, **You have memorized Scripture by setting it to music. Advertisers know that music helps us memorize as we sing the appealing phrases over and over again. Bible memory is not the only thing that needs repetition. We also need to repeat to ourselves that God will take care of our companionship needs. What do you want in companionship—someone to share your life with?** Invite a fast-writing youth to write answers on a chalkboard or paper. (Samples: Someone to talk to, someone who understands me, someone I can understand, someone to share dreams with, a partner in reaching those dreams.) Stress, **God cares about companionship. He created us with a need for it. Who will read Genesis 2:18?** Pause to listen as a youth reads it.

Point out, **Verses like these show that God is not the only need we have but God is the first need we have.** Demonstrate this by giving each youth a copy of Handout 11, which you have cut apart and placed in separate business-size envelopes (or paper clip each set of pieces together if you have no envelopes handy). Direct youth to take out the large rectangle and then search for the one piece that fits the hole in the middle (the one labeled *God*). As youth find the piece, agree that God is the only one who can fill the empty space within us and that a man named Pascal is said to have spoken of this God-shaped vacuum. Then say, **Even though it's true that only God can fill the empty place inside us, most people try to**

SESSION 7

Bonus Option

Give each youth a huge rock and guide them to paint phrases from Matthew 6:19–21, 25–34 that encourage them to turn their worries into work, their groans into goals, their pain into prayer. Provide newspapers, fine-tipped brushes, and paints. Then urge youth to write their worries and put them under this rock to remind them that God's power is strong enough to help them discover just what to do about each worry. Urge them to add new worries as they come about and remove old worries as they are solved.

fill the emptiness with other things. Choose several shapes from your envelope and try to fill your empty place with them. Write your own ideas on the blank shapes. Circulate and comment that the other pieces fall through. Notice if one youth discovers that by placing them just right he can cover the hole with several of the shapes. Go to that youth and say, **This wise person has discovered that there is a way to cover the hole. There are no empty spaces visible. This rectangle looks complete. But when hard times come, as they do to every person** (shake the rectangle so the shapes fall through the hole), **these other things fall right through.** Put the *God* piece in this youth's rectangle, hold it in place, and say, **But when God is the foundation, all these other things are added.** Invite this youth and his neighbors to add on pieces. Then shake the foundation and see that some fall off but *God* stays steady. Ask,

- **How have you seen God be your unshakable foundation?**
- **How has putting God first given stability to another area of your life such as a boyfriend/girlfriend, good grades, money, food, friends, clothing, family, living arrangements, or interesting work?** Encourage responses to each of these.
- **How has unhappiness resulted when you put another area before God?**

Stress again, **Friends, boyfriends, girlfriends, family, grades, money, food, interesting work, and other things are important. The key to happiness is to let God be the organizing force to all of them, the hub in the middle.** Pray, thanking God for guiding our lives. Invite one youth to read Matthew 6:32–33 while the others keep their heads bowed. Suggest they keep the rectangles in their Bibles as a reminder to live these verses.

Step 3: Worry with a Reason (10–15 minutes)

Teasingly say, **So now that we know this verse, are all our dating worries over?** Remind the youth that being a Christian does not mean our worries are over, but it does mean we have God's power to manage our worries. Distribute paper and pencils. Direct youth to write, with pencil, worries they have about dating and marriage, perhaps the same ones they prayed about in Step 1. Explain that this worry sheet will be private, that you will invite youth to speak from it but will force no one.

Second, give a fine-tipped marking pen to each youth and direct them to write next to each worry a phrase from Matthew 6:19–21, 25–34 that gives them comfort in or help with this worry. Third, direct youth to get a new color marking pen and write an action or attitude that will help solve this worry. As youth work, explain, **Worry is one of the main things we do in dating. The best way to worry is to worry long enough to figure out what to do about it.** Add also that in this Matthew passage, Jesus scolds His listeners for worrying about certain things, not for worrying period. Circulate to help youth as they write. Allow them to ask advice from one another. After youth have completed all three writings, highlight the colors on the page, saying that when we talk to God about our worries, He sheds new insight on how to solve them. Invite each youth to tell about one worry, one helpful Bible phrase, and one solution. Force no one, in keeping with your promise. Samples include

"What if I never get a girlfriend?"	Your heavenly Father knows that you need them (v. 32).	I'll remember that God knows I need companionship, and He knows what is best for me.
"What if I marry someone who beats me?"	Where your treasure is, there will your heart be also (v. 21).	I'll watch the way dates treat me now and avoid any hints of violence or hurt-and-then-apologize cycles. I'll also look where his treasure is. And I'll treasure character, not looks.
"What if she turns me down if I ask her out?"	Seek first His kingdom and His righteousness, and all these things will be given (v. 33).	Even if she never likes me back, someone else will. She might like me a lot already, but if I don't ask, I could miss a lot, so I'm going to ask God for courage to ask her.
"My parents are divorced; what if I get divorced?"	Each day has enough trouble of its own (v. 34).	I'll worry about today mainly but I'll also decide to deliberately learn different patterns since I'll be prone toward divorce.
"What will I wear?"	Is not life more important than food, and the body more important than clothes? (v. 25)	Though I want to look nice, it's more important that I act nice—making my date feel comfortable around me.

Invite youth to summarize in one sentence how they will let God help them with their dating worries. Samples might include
- when I start to worry, I'll start talking to God about it;
- rather than feel guilty about worry, I'll turn worry into thinking and then into action;
- when I worry, I'll discover what can be done to help fix the worry.

SESSION 7

Teacher Tip

Many believe affirmation activities like this one will make youth self-centered. But affirmation activities actually help youth discover specific reasons God has created them likeable. Such activities also reinforce for youth the idea that people really do care for them. Third, it gives youth practice encouraging one another as directed by Hebrews 10:24–25. Thank youth for building each other up. Instead of a room full of big heads, you'll have humble youth equipped to care.

Step 4: Whack One Worry (10 minutes)

Point out, **One worry that bothers almost every teenager is looks. "Do I look okay?" "Why did my hair go this way today?" "Will I ever be attractive enough to get a date?"** Emphasize that God makes *every* person attractive, and we honor Him when we look for that in ourselves. This is not conceit but letting God's good work give us confidence. When we believe we look good, we relax enough to care well.

Add, **One important truth in looking for God's good work is to see the variety in the way He gives good looks.** To show the variety in good looks tell these stories:

Tony is the life of the party. He tells jokes that keep everyone laughing. His tousled hair and freckles give him that mischievous look that's so attractive.

Gina has a compliment for everyone. She makes you feel important by listening to and understanding your feelings. Her dark eyes and naturally curly hair are as intense as she is.

Rhea is quiet in a group. Every new day delights and challenges her. She watches for a fresh bit of understanding wherever she goes. The simple things take on a whole new meaning when Rhea is around. Her long hair and deep blue eyes are sensitive like she is.

Ask, **How is each person beautiful? Look around at each person here. How is each beautiful?** Direct each youth to write his or her first name vertically down the side of an index card and then pass it to the left. That person writes one attractive quality beginning with one letter of the name. Urge youth to name a way that quality is attractive such as "Your eyes sparkle" rather than "Nice eyes." Pass again to the left and repeat. Do this about five times, circulating to make sure no one writes ugly remarks. Pass these back to the original owners and give a minute to read them. Then urge each youth to privately write two things they like about their own appearance and how to use it for God. (Samples: I have a nice smile; I can make people feel at home with it. I'm tall; I can do chores on high shelves.) Urge youth, **Each time you look in the mirror, spot one element of God's good work in you and thank God for it.**

Live What You Learn

Step 5:
Climb Out of Self-Pity
(10 minutes)

Warn youth, **Whether your dating worry is looks, finding someone good, or growing close to the one you've found, refuse to fall into the pit of feeling sorry for yourself. Instead realize you have the power of almighty God to help you. Together you and God can solve problems. When you find yourself worrying, pray and ask God to lead you to discover what to do and how to do it.** Urge youth to summarize the biblical way to worry by completing this sentence, which you have written on the chalkboard:

Worry is good when _____, but worry is bad
when _____.

(Samples: Worry is good when we let it prompt us to actions and attitudes that help, but worry is bad when we fret and do nothing. Worry is good when we invite God to help us figure out what to do, but worry is bad when we feel sorry for ourselves. Worry is good when we worry about changing a bad habit or getting out of a destructive dating relationship, but worry is bad when we worry about clothing and food. Worry is good when someone or something needs attention, but worry is bad when that problem is already taken care of.) Together with youth thank God for caring about the details in our lives. Ask Him to help them be patient as He works out His dating plans in their lives.

find the mistakes

Circle and correct each mistake in this retelling of Matthew 6:19–21, 25–34. Work with a partner. One of you read the Bible passage aloud from the New International Version of the Bible while the other finds and corrects the mistakes.

Store up for yourselves treasures on earth, keeping them safe in a box, and where thieves can't get them. But store up for yourselves treasures in the bank, where moth and rust do not destroy, and where only some thieves break in and steal. For where your treasure is, there you will be rich. ... Therefore I tell you, worry about your life, what you will say or do; or about your body, what you will wear. Is not food more important than life, and clothes more important than the body? Look at the birds of the air; they do not sow or reap or store away in barns, and yet your heavenly Father feeds them. Are you not much less valuable than they? Who of you by worrying can add a single hour to his life? And why do you worry about status? See how the lilies of the field grow. They do not labor or spin. Yet I tell you that not even Solomon in all his splendor was dressed like one of these. If that is how God clothes the grass of the field, which is gorgeous to look at, will He not much more clothe you, O you of little faith? So do not worry, saying, 'What shall we eat?' or 'What shall we drink?' or 'What shall we wear?' For the holy run after all these things, and your heavenly Father fusses at them for it. But seek last His kingdom and His riches, and all these things will be withheld from you as well. Therefore do not worry about tomorrow, for tomorrow will worry about itself. Each day has enough trouble of its own.

HANDOUT 11 — SESSION 7

God-Shaped Empty Place

"Your heavenly Father knows that you need them. But seek first His kingdom and His righteousness, and all these things will be given to you as well (Matthew 6:32-33)."

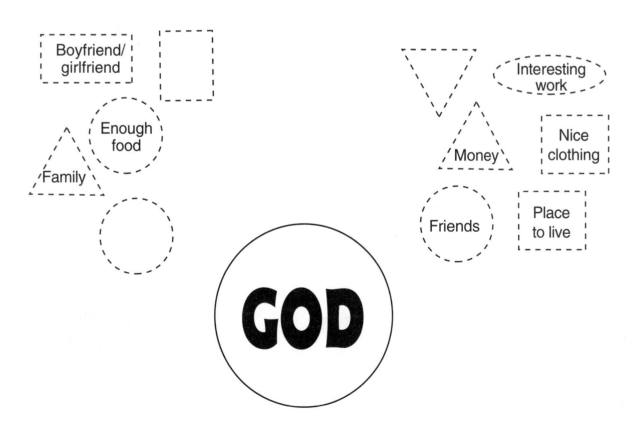

Psalm 37:1–8; Philippians 2:1–5

SESSION 8

How Can I Tell Her I Want to Break Up?

Focus on a Goal Truth

Kindly but firmly end relationships that don't have the four pillars of faith, respect, enjoyment, and mutuality.

Understand Concerns Youth Have

- I don't want to hurt her feelings. How can I tell her I want to break up?
- Isn't it best to back off slowly?
- Why can't I just date one person and never have to break up?

Connect Scripture to Youth Concerns

1. Demonstrate how pillars give relationships strength to last.
2. List actions that make it easier to receive or give a breakup.
3. Generate ideas that will avoid the need for a breakup.

Gather Supplies and Prepare

- Bring extra Bibles, pencils, paper, marking pens, and masking tape.
- Bring a variety of pillars and rectangles. Three sample sets include a book balanced on four building blocks, an index card balanced on four toothpicks, a box balanced on four inflated balloons.
- Photocopy Handout 12, one per youth.
- Cut and bring credit card-sized paper, preferably cut from poster board.
- Bring construction paper in various colors.
- Bring mousetraps with the snap bar removed if you choose the Bonus Option.

SESSION 8

Invite Attention

Step 1: Find Four Pillars (10 minutes)

As youth enter, give teams of two or more youth a set of four pillars and a rectangle to balance on top. Give each team a different type of pillar and rectangle to compare the nature of pillars and foundations in relationships. These discussion questions will be based on the three examples listed above; adapt the questions to match the pillars you bring. Challenge youth, **Balance your rectangle foundation by placing the four pillars under its corners. See what you can stack on top of the foundation, such as other books, purses, shoes, and more. Then see what happens if you remove one of the four pillars or when you rearrange the pillars.** Invite youth to discuss their findings with questions like

- **How well did your four pillars support your foundation?**
- **What happened when you took one of the pillars away from the corners?**
- **What happened when you moved a pillar toward the center?**
- **Looking at other groups' pillar materials, what combination seems to make the best pillars for foundation and for the things you stack on top?**

Encourage youth to voice a variety of insights such as the following: The building blocks provided the best support because they had a broad base and didn't fall down. In all the structures four supports widely spaced gave the strongest foundation. The balloons had good bounce, but you couldn't trust how the foundation would react on top of them. The toothpicks worked well on the carpet because they dug in, but when we tried to stack things on them, they broke. You could get away with three pillars but it was pretty wobbly. With two pillars things fell over. Then guide youth to respond to **What does this exercise say about pillars in a guy/girl relationship and the foundation you can build on those pillars?** (Samples: We need four pillars for the most stable relationships. The broader the pillars, the better they support life.) **In real life the relationship is the foundation (represented here by the book or paper or box) and the events of life are stacked on that relationship. How does that work? How does the relationship support the events of life?** (Samples: The stronger the pillars, the better the foundation can support life. Strong pillars make it easier to build a strong relationship. The relationship has to rest soundly on the pillars or it will fall when the pressures of life come. Even the most loving relationship can't support the events of life if it doesn't have good pillars.)

Stress, **Without four good pillars a relationship cannot last or be happy. Lifelong love must have a foundation firmly built on four supporting pillars. Let's name these: (1) faith, (2) respect, (3) enjoyment, (4) mutuality.** Invite youth, **Talking about one pillar at a time, tell me why the absence of that pillar would hurt a relationship.** Samples:

1. **Faith.** Without faith, one or both of us is not in touch with the source of truth who is God Himself. Then we would be living a lie and in conflict with each other.
2. **Respect.** Strong relationships must have mutual respect. If I don't respect my husband, I'll treat him as less valuable than me and vice versa. Respect breeds trust which breeds concern which breeds all that closeness is made of.
3. **Enjoyment.** I've got to like and be attracted to the person I marry or we won't have fun together. Delighting in each other is a strong foundation to shared life. I can respect and share faith with many people, but I want to live with the one I enjoy the most.
4. **Mutuality.** I can give respect, enjoy the person, and live faithfully to God but if she doesn't do these things with me, we have no relationship. In a strong relationship each partner must give as much as he takes, must listen as much as he speaks, must support as much as he is supported. Neither is slave of the other, but both are servants of each other.

Stress, **No matter how much you like someone, you can't build a true foundation of love without these four pillars supporting you. Without faith, respect, enjoyment, and mutuality a relationship will end or be sad. What other pillars do you believe are important to a strong love foundation?** (Samples might include things in common, shared values, etc.) The conclusion you want youth to draw is that attraction alone isn't enough to build love. Then say, **When you see that you and the one you date do not share adequate pillars to build love, it's time for a breakup.** Pause for a moment of silent prayer, urging youth to talk with God privately about when to breakup, how to handle it when it happens, and what actions to take to avoid the necessity of a breakup.

Dig into the Bible

Step 2: Walk through the Changes Others Bring (10–15 minutes)

With Handout 12, invite youth to tell what they dislike and appreciate about breaking up. If your group is larger than six, guide youth to share

SESSION 8

Teacher Tip

As youth make their lists, discourage them from assuming the one breaking up with them is evil. Instead, urge them to see it as a team process, all of us trying to find the right person, and that a breakup signals the need to try another match. At the same time, avoid the assumption that breakups are to be taken lightly. An easy-come-easy-go attitude encourages a lighthearted approach to dating and marriage, followed by the shock of how much a split hurts. Work for balancing "the connections in our lives matter" with "during dating we may have to change our connections to be sure that we can make a lifetime connection during marriage." A question to ponder: **What's the difference between a breakup and a divorce?**

answers in teams of up to six, giving a reason with each answer. Let the sheet prompt understanding and discussion, rather than simple reporting of answers. Say, **Breaking up is no fun, but there are ways to make it better. Let's focus first on being broken up with, and later we'll focus on doing the breaking up. Search Psalm 37:1–8 to create a tip list for coping with a breakup. Work in teams of about three to find a fun way to present your list, perhaps as a list of "Thou shalts" and "Thou shalt nots." Put the verse next to each tip.** Samples include

- Thou shalt not fret even if the person has done evil (37:1);
- Thou shalt focus on responding kindly rather than envying wrongdoing (37:1);
- Thou shalt realize that mean words will eventually fade (37:2);
- Thou shalt listen to all the breaker-upper has to say, asking God to help you understand (37:3);
- Thou shalt remember the good you shared (37:3);
- Thou shalt be comforted by God who keeps you safe (37:3).
- Thou shalt resist the temptation to never risk love again, and instead ask God to bring you delight even after a breakup (37:4);
- Thou shalt ask God to help you discover what to do next, to see any changes you might need in yourself to build a new relationship that brings the desires of the heart (37:4);
- Thou shalt commit to do right, no matter how mean the one breaking up is (37:5);
- Thou shalt trust that doing right works out well in the end and be willing to wait through the feelings of disappointment, heartbreak, and sorrow to see the good (37:6);
- Thou shalt cry and be still with God, your ultimate comforter (37:7);
- Thou shalt turn your anger into talking to God and to people who care (37:8);
- Thou shalt refrain from revenge, aloofness, or pride (37:8).

Invite youth to read their tip lists and then post them on the wall. Distribute credit card-sized papers and guide youth to write Psalm 34:18 on it: *The LORD is close to the brokenhearted and saves those who are crushed in spirit.* Say, **A credit card gives you buying power. What can you "buy" with this Bible truth?** (Samples: I can buy *comfort* because I have God's shoulder to cry on. I can buy *hope* because God assures me I am His child. I can buy *relaxation* because God knows I hurt and it's okay to hurt for awhile. I can buy *security* because God will always love me. I can buy *understanding* of whether to get back with this person after we both change a bit or whether to move on to someone else.) Assure youth that they never go through a breakup alone. Urge them to keep the card with their money as a promise they can bank on.

Step 3: Courageously Make Changes That Are Needed
(10 minutes)

Invite youth, **Now we'll make a second list for the one doing the breaking up.** Direct trios of youth to make another list of tips using Philippians 2:1–5. Samples include

- Thou shalt encourage the person by telling reasons you are glad you dated (2:1).
- Thou shalt not keep dating someone who does not draw encouragement and comfort from Christ (2:1).
- Thou shalt give comfort by telling the exact reasons you're breaking up rather than making the other guess (2:1). (For example, "Your fiery temper is one reason we can't go on. I'd rather talk out problems than yell about them. Yelling and throwing frighten me, and the last time you hit me. Since we bring out the worst in each other, it's best that we stop dating.")
- Thou shalt show tenderness and compassion by concentrating on your problems rather than the other's (2:1). (For example, "You've done nothing to make me feel this way, in fact I really like being around you. It's just that I feel restless. I have to settle it before I'm ready to commit.")
- Thou shalt honestly say when you discover lack of like-mindedness (2:2). (For example, "We don't agree on basic things of life such as children, the kinds of jobs we want, and how to spend our free time. I'm very attracted to you, but we can't build a relationship without more.")
- Thou shalt not be selfish in a breakup, like breaking up to date someone of higher status who will help you achieve an ambition (2:3).
- Thou shalt do what's right for the other person as well as for you (2:4).
- Thou shalt realize that doing right for the other person doesn't mean letting him or her hurt you or bring you down (2:4).
- Thou shalt break up with someone if the relationship is not mutual, that is if you or the other person is doing everything or the relationship is co-dependent (2:4).
- Thou shalt ask, "Would Jesus say or do this?" (2:5).

Stress, **In a breakup look out not only for your own interests but the interests of others as it says in Philippians 2:4.** Read Philippians 2:6–11 with the students. It is Paul's explanation for the advice given in 2:1–5. Pray for courage to imitate Christ's humility.

SESSION 8

Live What You Learn

Step 4:
Recognize Real Love
(10–15 minutes)

Transition with **Now that we have these lists, when do we use them? How do you know when it's time for a breakup?** Ask the question from the other side: **How can you tell you should stay together? Choose one of the four pillars (faith, respect, enjoyment, mutuality) and tell how you'd know it was missing or present.**

Invite youth to write situations about breaking up. Then guide youth to roleplay how to do these with guy/girl pairs. Suggest they play two versions: (1) the way it's usually handled; (2) the way Jesus wants us to handle it. Samples include

- We fight all the time. Does this mean we need to break up or we need to learn to get along better? What should I say in either case?
- I hoped this person would become a Christian. But it hasn't happened. How can I break up without giving the impression that Christians are snobby or exclusive?
- I went out those first few times because I didn't want to hurt his feelings. I was never that interested. But my date is getting very interested. How can I say that I didn't mean to lead this person on?
- This person really pushes me for sex. I've committed to wait until marriage but we keep going further and further. I know we have to break up before I do something I regret. What should I say?
- My date hits me. I don't want to be abused in marriage. How can I break up?
- I like someone else. It's that simple and that complicated. How can I assure this person that there's nothing wrong with her, I just want to date someone else?

Use youth's words to explain that even when a breakup is the right thing to do, it will hurt for awhile. Feeling lonely after a breakup doesn't mean the breakup was the wrong thing to do but that we miss companionship. The kinder and more direct we are in our dating and breaking up the less permanent damage we do. Discuss further with **What are ways to avoid a breakup—to recognize the four pillars (faith, respect, enjoyment, mutuality) in a person before you even go out on one date?**

Step 5: Avoid the Traps (10 minutes)

Say, **Even when we know the pillars to watch for, and even when we want a healthy dating relationship, we sometimes let ourselves get trapped in unhappy dating situations. Why?** Display construction paper in various colors. Invite youth to think about a friend who has gotten into a destructive dating relationship and choose a color that pictures the experience. Ask,

- **What traps do people walk into in dating and what color are these traps?** Invite youth to tell about the color they chose and why, being careful not to mention the name or identifying details. (Sample traps include dating someone who abuses you, rebounding after a breakup, picking up dates you don't know, dating someone you feel sorry for, trying to make someone better, equating sex with love, dating non-Christians.)
- **Why do we think we can nibble on the cheese of a trap without getting caught in it?** (Sample answers include the following: We think we can help someone change. Movies tell us that if we're "ready," sex outside marriage is fine. Meeting a good-looking stranger seems romantic. We believe bad things won't happen.)
- **What happens when the trap snaps, as it invariably will?** (Sample answers include a miserable dating relationship that leads to a worse marriage, date rape, pain that haunts us, a breakup we didn't intend.)
- **What makes us put up with bad treatment just to have a boyfriend or girlfriend?** (Sample answers include the following: We are made to need companionship so we blind our eyes to what's good. We spend too much time alone and grow vulnerable. We falsely believe dates give us value.)
- **What strategies will help us avoid the traps and find the treasures instead?** (Sample answers include the following: Realize when we're vulnerable. Make lots of friends of both sexes so the loneliness isn't as intense. Commit to wait until marriage for sex. Realize that evangelistic dating seldom works. Date only people I already know. Look for quality people. Go out in groups of both guys and girls. Be happy in who I am. Invite God's power to do all this.)

Say, **Healthy dating and breaking up is not easy. But through these experiences you can build happy, lasting, and exciting relationships. You can avoid the traps. You can have the cheese without the trap coming down on your head. Trust yourself and obey your God.**

Bonus Option

Enhance Step 5 by giving each youth a wooden mouse trap from which you've removed the snap bar so it cannot be set. Direct youth to write on the top a trap that could lead them into dating pain (see samples under Step 5). Provide Sharpie marking pens. Then on the bottom, direct youth to write at least three strategies for avoiding this trap. Discuss with the questions in Step 5.

BREAKUP FEELINGS

Choose one or more of these responses and tell why you feel that way.

When someone breaks up with me, I hate it when (or I'd hate it if)
- he or she just pulls back without telling me what's going on;
- he or she pretends like it's no big deal or the relationship didn't matter;
- he or she lets someone else tell me;
- _____.

When someone breaks up with me, I appreciate it when (or I'd appreciate it if)
- he or she tells me why our relationship mattered rather than brush it all aside;
- he or she cries or seems a little sad about it;
- he or she gives me a little space to recover rather than tries to be friends right away;
- _____.

When I break up with someone, I worry that
- I will hurt him or her;
- the good we had together will die—I want good to live on;
- I won't say the things that show how truly sorry I am;
- _____.

When I break up with someone, I really want to
- know I'm doing the right thing;
- show that person how glad I am that we dated;
- glorify God in what I say and do;
- _____.

Psalm 1; Ephesians 3:14–21

SESSION 9

What's the Best Way to Pick a Mate?

Focus on a Goal Truth

You make the best choices for marriage when you let trustworthy people—friends and parents and caring church members—help you.

Understand Concerns Youth Have

- Is there something less painful than dating and breaking up and dating again?
- Why is finding the right one so hard?
- Where are all the quality people?

Connect Scripture to Youth Concerns

1. Discuss possible alternatives to dating and how to access advantages of each.
2. Illustrate godly character.
3. Develop strategies to finding real love: recognize it, wait for it, look nearby.

Gather Supplies and Prepare

- Bring extra Bibles, pencils, paper, marking pens, and masking tape.
- Photocopy one copy of Handout 13, cut apart the four signs, display one per wall.
- Remove all the chairs from the room (or stack them in a corner) to encourage the walking discussion.
- Bring clay pots, plants, paints, and brushes if you choose the Bonus Option.

SESSION 9

- Photocopy and cut apart one copy of Handout 14 for each youth.
- Bring plastic adhesive bandages and ballpoint pens.

Invite Attention

Step 1: Is There a Better Way than Dating? (15–20 minutes)

Guide a walking discussion about good ways to find a lifelong match. To begin, remove all the chairs from the room and remind the students, **In Session 8 we talked about the pain of breaking up. Nobody likes to break up, so could there be a better option to dating and breaking up, a way to find one person and keep that one? I'll make a statement and you go to the sign on the wall that tells how you feel about it. Then we'll discuss it.** Point out the signs *Agree, Disagree, Strongly Agree, Strongly Disagree* cut from Handout 13 that you have displayed on four walls. After reading each of the following statements, direct youth to choose a sign to stand by. If they feel torn between two, urge them to move to the one that most closely matches their feelings and then, when called on, explain why they feel two ways.

Move to the smallest group to affirm their courage to stand alone or in a smaller crowd. Ask one or two in that group to tell why they *agree* (or whatever sign they're standing under) that betrothal is a better option than dating (or whatever statement you are currently discussing). Move to the next largest group, the next, and finally to the largest. Harmonize statements by highlighting something wise from each area of the room. Ask all youth to walk back to the center of the room and choose again for the next statement. Repeat the discussion process. Each statement has discussion prompter ideas in parentheses:

- **Better than dating would be betrothal, a match made by parents that is as binding as a marriage.** (Because parents know their kids well, they could gather with other parents and make matches based on personality and interests. They could invite the help of their teenagers in making these matches. This was the way matches were made by many Bible families. This could be bad if parents don't know their kids. Parents could make matches for the wrong motives just like youth.)
- **Better than dating would be courtship, where a guy gets permission from the girl's parents to court the girl and visits the girl in her home.** (Because the couple sees each other mainly in the home of the girl, they would find out how they liked each other in everyday

SESSION 9

circumstances. Because you marry the family, you could find out what the family is like. Because the parents are home but not in the room with them, the couple would have less sexual temptation. Because some parents would not be helpful, the teenagers might get to know each other better in other ways. Dates need to see each other more than at home, such as in groups.)

- **Better than dating would be waiting until you're ready to marry and then dating one person you're interested in marrying to see how compatible you are.** (This relationship could still have a breakup. Even though you're more mature, you might miss something. Many people want to have fun dating before marriage. Its advantage is you have more time to know people as friends to see the kind of person you want to marry.)
- **Better than dating would be to go out in groups and then pick someone from that group.** (Groups offer opportunity to see how the one you like treats other people. It is also good life practice because real life is more with groups than just with the two of you. We all long for time alone with special people.)
- **Better than dating would be to let your church leaders match you with someone you're similar to.** (Explain that some churches and cults believe this is best. Caution against it because few church leaders could know you well enough to make a good match.)
- **Better than dating would be to _____ .** (Encourage volunteers to fill in other matching possibilities. Help that youth lead the whole room discussion on the topic.)

Discuss the entire exercise with **Even if you don't give up dating, how might you bring aspects of these other options into your dating?** Encourage much discussion of the pros and cons of each selection method. Samples:

- *Betrothal:* We could invite our parents' opinions on the people we're interested in dating. After we start dating, we could continue to ask their help and advice on specific circumstances.
- *Courtship:* It would be good to spend lots of time in each other's homes with our parents around. Family time also would help us know each other better.
- *Waiting until you're ready to marry:* We could focus on friendships now so the sexual pressures wouldn't be so great. We could know more people that way.
- *Go out in groups:* We could see more sides of the one we date if we go out in groups at least some of the time.
- *Church leaders:* I could ask leaders I trust to assess who might be good for me or to tell me how a person I'm currently dating is impacting me.

Teacher Tip

Let this walking discussion bring out the many facets of finding and choosing a mate. It's like a diamond that we examine from each side to see a different sparkle or cut. Rather than imply that one side "wins" during each round, show how each side is showing a different aspect of the same truth—**we must look carefully at a person's character to make certain we are well matched before marriage.**

SESSION 9

Dig into the Bible

Step 2:
Seek Someone Righteous
(10 minutes)

Guide youth to illustrate godly character. To do this, transition by saying, **No matter how you find one another, your goal is to find someone godly, like a tree planted by water.** Challenge youth to find this description in Psalm 1 and discuss the advantages of a tree like this (strong because of its deep roots, giving because of its steady supply of new nourishment, constantly growing because of its location). Ask, **What is a person of strong character like?** Ask each youth to say one word that describes good character. Guide youth to read Psalm 1 and Ephesians 3:14–21 for some of these words. (Samples: steady, true, Christlike, powerful, genuine, hard-working, kind, understanding, cooperative, encouraging.)

Then guide youth to reread Psalm 1 and Ephesians 3:14–21 to draw a caricature or political cartoon of the person they want to marry and of the one they don't want to marry, labeled with characteristics from these Bible passages. Tell the youth that a caricature is a sketch with exaggerated features, and a political cartoon includes symbols that tell the story. Suggest that youth might draw someone with feet down deep in the Bible and an apple hanging off a thumb to show that the person will draw nourishment from God so they can bear fruits of kindness and love. Youth could label both the feet and thumb with Psalm 1:3 or Ephesians 3:17. Youth might also mark increments on the person like on a measuring cup to show they want someone full of the measure of the fullness of God. They'd label this Ephesians 3:19. For the one youth don't want to marry, youth might draw a person being lured by money to show they don't want someone easily influenced by greed. They would label this drawing with Psalm 1:4. Provide paper and marking pens.

As youth show their cartoons, use their words to emphasize **Character is much more valuable than cuteness. How can character become as attractive to us as looks? What character trait do you find really attractive?** Youth may more easily recognize the term *personality* than *character* so explain that character is good personality, a personality that does the right thing no matter how hard. As youth talk about an attractive character, they will discover that other youth value character, which will prompt them to value character.

SESSION 9

Step 3:
See True Love
(10 minutes)

Explain, **Every now and then the first person someone dates becomes the person he or she marries. But most often there's a series of relationships that leads to a permanent one.** Invite youth to tell the story of how their parents (or other adults they know) met and married. It might go something like this:

> Samantha met a guy named Stephen, and they became fast friends. He liked her for a long time, but just about the time she became interested in him, he started to date someone else. In the meantime, Samantha met a guy named Sam at youth camp. First attracted by their same names, they wrote letters and sent e-mail messages. When they later got together in person, they found they weren't as compatible as they thought. In fact, Sam was physically and verbally abusive to Samantha. So Samantha cut that relationship off quickly and spent two years without a boyfriend. It was lonely, but she coped by spending time with her extraordinary girlfriends. She met Tad when they both got summer jobs at the place where their parents worked. Friends first, they went out after work frequently. Soon both recognized there was more to their relationship. Today they have three busy daughters.

Emphasize, **No matter how you choose the one you will marry, recognizing good character is a must—Samantha dropped Sam like a hot potato when she recognized his abusive tendencies.** Ask youth to repeat one word that describes good character, recalling Step 2. Then invite them to practice recognizing good character like this. Give each youth a set of six signs cut from Handout 14. Direct them to display these face up in their laps. Say, **I'm going to read statements that are often attributed to love. When I count to three, you hold up the sign that tells what is actually the root feeling behind the statement. All of you lift your signs at the same time to keep from watching others' choices.** Read a statement, look at youths' signs, then invite youth to translate the statement into love or a response that shows love. Sample sign answers are in parentheses and sample translations follow but listen for other possibilities also.

- **I'm the kind of person who needs a boyfriend all the time.** (fear, dependence) Possible translation—I like guys, but I don't need one to define my value.
- **If you leave me, I'll kill myself.** (control, fear) Possible response—If you need me to stay alive, our relationship doesn't have the foundation it needs.

Bonus Option

Give each youth a clay pot and direct them to paint on the side the words of Ephesians 3:17–19 or Psalm 1:2–3. Then help them plant a small fruit tree or flowering house plant in the pot. If they choose a flowering plant rather than a fruit tree, urge them to compare the flowers to fruit as they watch their plants grow over the weeks and months ahead. Discuss, **What does this plant need to grow? Will love alone make it grow?** (No, but love helps us give it what it needs.) **How is this plant like choosing and growing a love relationship? What Bible truth will it remind you of each time you see it?**

SESSION 9

- **I'm glad you like to cook and clean because I need someone to take care of me.** (control, using, dependence) Possible response—I'd rather be treated like a person, not a housemaid.
- **I had to go out with him because I didn't want to hurt his feelings.** (pity) Possible translation—The loving thing to do is turn him down from the first. Then I won't lead him on.
- **I know she's not a Christian, but I may be the only one who helps her become one.** (pity, using) Possible translation—It's usually better that girls witness to girls and guys to guys to avoid the romance factor complicating things.
- **I like to have a girl on my arm.** (dependence, using) Possible translation—I like girls as people, not accessories.
- **I love him so I have to show it by going to bed with him.** (using, dependence) Possible translation—Because I love him, I'll wait until marriage for sex; if he pushes, he's using me, not loving me.

Invite youth to talk to God, telling Him why they commit to find real love, not imitations.

Step 4:
Endure—Even Enjoy—the Wait
(5–10 minutes)

Agree that we'd all love to be growing close to someone, but we may not yet see the one God wants for us. Ask, **How do we wait? With your group, write on these bandages actions that can ease the hurt of waiting.** Provide plastic adhesive bandages and ballpoint pens to write on them. As each youth tells about a bandage, direct the others to add these ideas to their bandages. Direct each youth to mark Psalm 1 in their Bibles with this many-idea bandage. Pray together for God's wisdom as we date and wait.

Ask, **What action or attitude would you *not* want in your bandage supply—things people try that actually make the wait worse?** (Samples: Give sex. Date someone you really don't like. Attempt suicide. Have self-pity. Assume you're the only one with this problem.)

Live What You Learn

Step 5:
Don't Ignore the Ones Already in Your Path
(10 minutes)

Suggest, **Sometimes we overlook the very best choices for a mate by forgetting to consider our friends of the opposite sex. Let's practice recognizing the good in the Christian people we already know.** Give youth paper and direct them to spread as far apart as your room allows. Then say, **On this paper, write a letter to a friend of the opposite sex telling what you like about him or her and why it might be fun to be married to this friend. This doesn't mean you will marry and you won't give this letter to the friend. It's practice in seeing the good God creates.** Circulate and encourage youth. After a few minutes invite volunteers to read a characteristic that they wrote about in the letter, with no identifying details on who the friend is. (Samples might include the following: You listen to what I have to say. I'm comfortable around you. Your faith is so natural. We have fun together uncomplicated by the nervousness of dating. You tell me your dreams. You never put me or anyone else down.) Guide youth to tear up the letters in tiny bits and bring them to the trash sack you are holding in the middle of the group. Explain that they can rewrite the letter later, but that you don't want a chance of others reading their private thoughts. If youth want to keep their letters that is fine. Urge youth to put the letters in a safe place.

Stress, **Finding and growing close to the person who becomes your mate is the most important choice you'll make. Let's invite God's help with this.** Ask each youth to add a sentence to this prayer for wisdom, courage, and sensitivity. Close with something like this: God, help us to recognize godly character in the person or persons You want us to grow close to, in just the way You want it to happen.

Agree/Disagree Signs

Disagree	Strongly Disagree
Agree	Strongly Agree

HANDOUT 14 — SESSION 9

Love or Not Signs

Fear	**Pity**
Control	**Dependence**
Love	**Using**

Ephesians 5:21–33

SESSION 10

Guys Earn the Money, Girls Keep the House—Or Do They?

Focus on a Goal Truth

Love looks at roles and expectations before you commit to marry each other. It talks out needs and hopes rather than expecting the other person to *know* your thoughts and feelings.

Understand Concerns Youth Have

- I hate to do dishes so I'll just let my husband do that.
- That's the guy's job. Or, that's the woman's job.
- Does it really matter who does what?

Connect Scripture to Youth Concerns

1. Examine our current perceptions of roles.
2. See roles in the light of submitting to one another out of reverence for Christ.
3. Pinpoint specific actions that will help us work together in marriage

Gather Supplies and Prepare

- Bring extra Bibles, pencils, paper, and marking pens.
- Photocopy Handout 15, one copy for every two youth (on heavy paper if available) to simulate playing cards. Cut apart the sections.
- Consider photocopying and cutting apart the six case studies in Step 4.
- Provide paper and marking pens for doodling in Step 2 and for the maps in Step 5.

SESSION 10

Invite Attention

Step 1: Lay Your Expectations on the Table (15 minutes)

As youth enter, pair them, give them a set of eight role cards facedown from Handout 15, and direct them to briefly invent and play a game with the eight cards. When all have arrived, direct the pairs to shuffle and deal the cards evenly and then look at their hands. Ask, **Do you like the hand you were dealt? Why or why not? What card might you trade for something unseen in the other person's hand?** Direct youth to stop and do this as many times as they are willing, not showing what they trade but looking when they see what is given them. **How would you trade if you could see all the cards?** Direct the pairs to lay all cards down faceup in front of them, and trade until each has four roles they are willing to take. Discuss with

- **What game did you invent before I guided you in a trading game?**
- **How is taking what you were dealt like marriage? Is this the way God likes it?**
- **How is trading roles like marriage? Is it best when looking or not?**
- **If God were to choose the most important role for you, what would it be? Why?**

Use students' words to point out that too often couples go into marriage with unseen expectations and then become irritated with each other if those expectations aren't fulfilled. Or, they play games for which the other might not know the rules. Ask, **What examples can you give?** (Samples: One expects the other to earn all the money. One expects the other to do all the cooking.) **How can you avoid these problems in your marriages-to-be?** (Samples: Talk about expectations. Make sure your expectations match. Notice unspoken expectations. Watch the way his or her family members relate for a hint of what kind of communication he or she grew up with. Notice and refine your own expectations. Be aware of society's expectations. Tell what you want and need rather than expect the other to know or sense it.) Urge youth to openly talk about expectations since no one can read another person's mind. Assure them that expectations—and management of them—are an important part of how well they will get along in marriage.

Dig into the Bible

Step 2:
See True Love as an Everyday Thing
(10 minutes)

Say, **The church has taught us to have certain expectations of marriage. Some of these are what God expects; some are traditions people expect but God did not design. As we study Scripture, we can find and live up to God's true expectations.** Encourage youth to continually learn more from the Bible so they can grow closer to what God wants them to be in marriage and in other parts of life. Pause to pray that God will help them in this.

Direct youth to open their Bibles to Ephesians 5, a passage that can help them understand marriage roles and expectations. Open a brief discussion on the differences in role expectations between the first century and now. Remind students that Ephesians 5 says that the husband has the much weightier responsibility to love as Christ loves. (The usual emphasis is that the wife should submit.) Guide youth to memorize Ephesians 5:21 by assigning one word to each youth. If you have more than 10 youth, assign teams to the same word. Then have the youth/team call out each word in order. In the New International Version of the Bible it would sound like this:

Person 1: Submit

Person 2: to

Person 3: one

Person 4: another

Person 5: out

Person 6: of

Person 7: reverence

Person 8: for

Person 9: Christ.

Person 10: Ephesians 5:21

Repeat a second time, this time telling person 9 to sit down and be silent. Prompt the group to fill in the missing word, "Christ." Repeat several more times, seating a youth each time until the group is speaking the verse from memory. Ask, **How does this Bible command help us with expectations and roles in marriage?** (Samples: Mutuality prompts each of us to want to give to the other. Doing work and chores for Christ gives us motivation. Marriage is serving God because we do it for Jesus Christ.)

Explain that the *Holman Student Bible Dictionary* defines *submission* as "voluntary yielding in love" and "to consider the other's needs." Ask,

- **What is the difference between submission and slavery?**
- **What is the difference between submission and being a doormat?**

SESSION 10

- **What is the difference between submission and selfishness?**
- **Why would bossiness or abuse be distortions of biblical submission?**

Invite youth to give examples of the good that came when they submitted to someone or someone submitted to them.

Direct youth to read Ephesians 5:22–33 to find comparisons between marriage and the church. Suggest they doodle these comparisons on paper that you provide. Samples:

- A husband leads his wife as Christ leads the church. This is not bossy leading but a self-sacrificing leading that brings good to both (vv. 23–25).
- A wife voluntarily yields to her husband in love to bring good to both, like the way the church submits to Christ (vv. 22–24).
- A husband's care for his wife is to imitate the way God loves (vv. 25–31).
- A woman and man work, live, and show affection so lovingly that they become an inseparable union similar to Christ and the church (v. 31).
- Husbands and wives put their relationship first, not in a selfish way, but in a way that shows their new family is a priority (v. 31).
- It's as hard to put husband/wife love into words as it is to explain the mystery of Christ and the church (vv. 32–33).

Invite each youth to share a sample doodle. Agree that we write happiness in our lives by listening to God, understanding our spouse, and expressing love to both.

Step 3:
Let Love and Submission Help You Work Out Roles
(5–10 minutes)

Pull out one or two decks of Expectation Cards from Handout 15 as used in Step 1 and lay them face down in a pile. Direct youth in turn to pick one from the pile and tell how submission and love would respond to this expectation. The goal is to turn chores and responsibilities into ways to show love and submission. Samples:

- *Earning money:* Love and submission would work hard for my spouse and children.
- *Cleaning and household chores:* Submission and love recognize that splitting the yuck work is more caring than making the other person do it all.
- *Yardwork:* Submission and love might suggest doing it together, one mowing while the other trims bushes or edges. Or, one would do it for the sake of the other, knowing that he or she will take a turn the next time.

- *Shopping and cooking:* Submission and love would split these according to schedule and skill.
- *Caring for ill children:* Love and submission would get up in the middle of the night because it needs to be done and because it shows care for children.

Step 4:
Show Love in the Everyday
(10–15 minutes)

Say, **Expectations cause much conflict and sadness in marriage if they are not in harmony or are not worked out with mutual submission. An expectation is the assumption that the other is supposed to fulfill a specific role. Marital expectations include not only who takes care of which responsibility, but also how we want the other to act or change. Some expectations are fair and godly, some are not. An example of an unfair expectation is to assume a spouse will know what you're thinking or needing. Let's look at some specific cases and show ways to harmonize them with love and submission. With each case, name an attitude that would show love and submission, and then improvise a conversation for the group.** Pair youth and direct them to decide who will be the husband and the wife. Be sensitive to your group dynamic. Because your group may not divide evenly into pairs or some youth may be self-conscious working with the opposite sex, don't insist on opposite gender pairs. Remind students that the focus is on sharing love and submission with *another person*.

Case 1: Carl and Carla argue almost daily about taking out the garbage. Carl says his mom always took out the trash. Carla says her dad always took it out. Each assumes it's the other's job. How can Carl and Carla split up the nobody-likes-this-job jobs?

Case 2: Paul expects Paula to know what he's thinking and what he wants. "You should know I want some time to myself when I get home from work. Why do you insist on talking right away?" Paula expects the same from Paul, "After being away from each other all day, you should know I'm ready to talk!" How can Paul and Paula remember that neither can read minds, that they can simply say what they want, and work together to give what is asked of them. For example, Paula could wait 10 minutes and then Paul could be willing to talk.

Case 3: Vern really wants to stay home with their preschoolers but worries that people would see him as less of a man. Veronica loves both her job and her children but feels guilty about that. She thinks if she was a good mother she would want to be with her children all day.

SESSION 10

Bonus Option

Guide youth to develop a system for dividing the work of marriage. Samples:

- Write on cards all the work—household, decision, and yard chores—that need to be done and take turns picking cards until they're all gone.

- List attitudes and principles such as be willing to do more than your share; divide evenly all the "nobody likes" and "everybody likes" jobs; see communication as a job worth doing. Then apply those principles to specific situations.

But after working eight hours, she feels happy to see them. How can Vern and Veronica free themselves to give their children the parenting they need?

Case 4: Emil and Emily are so starry-eyed they assume they'll have no problem with expectations or roles. Unwilling to make the tough choices that role expectations bring, they're heading into marriage saying, "We'll both do that." Or, Emil says, "Emily won't mind doing that," while Emily says, "My husband will take care of that." How can they come up with realistic solutions?

Case 5: Dean assumes that Denise will do all the child care and housework, run all his errands for him, even make phone calls related to responsibilities he agrees to. Denise feels like he wants a servant rather than a helpmate. How would you guide Dean to recognize that honoring God means Dean gives to Denise and Denise gives to him? How would you help Dean and Denise if they haven't married yet? If they have?

Case 6: Duncan feels like all Dierdre does is sit around with the kids all day so she shouldn't ask for his help when he comes home. Dierdre feels like Duncan won't do his share of the household chores that still wait after her busy day of child care and homemaking. How can Dierdre see the pressures and pleasures Duncan faces at work? How can Duncan see the pressures and pleasures Dierdre faces as a stay-at-home mom?

Feel free to offer these sample attitudes as youth prepare to present their conversations (by case number): 1. Cooperation; 2. Communication, understanding; 3. Flexibility, honor God in the choices they make; 4. Reality, love other as self; 5. Love like Christ loves rather than selfishly; 6. Understanding, appreciation. In all six, encourage an attitude of loving, submission, realism, specificity, and continued honoring of God.

Live What You Learn

Step 5: Map Your Home (10 minutes)

Give each youth paper and marking pens and guide them in an open-eyed prayer process to digest everything they've discovered during this session. Say, **The Bible does not say that Susie is to do the dishes and Sam is to mow the lawn. So we work hand-in-hand with God to do the work of marriage. This obviously includes talking with God to find out His directions, personalized for us. Keeping in mind what**

SESSION 10

you've discovered from Scripture and the case studies we just discussed, **talk with God about how you will work out roles and expectations in your marriage. To do this draw a map of your current home, and invite God to help you draw or write in each room what His role would be for you as a spouse in that room.** Remind youth to focus on submission and love. Also, urge them to glean ideas from Ephesians 5, including verses 1–20. Samples might include the following:

- In the bathroom I'll wipe off the sink after I use it to make sure neither of us has to clean the bathroom much. I'll also refuse to spend so much time in there that my spouse can't get ready on time, in keeping with Ephesians 5:16.
- In the bedroom I will wake up cheerfully in keeping with Ephesians 5:14. The last one out of bed will make the bed. I'll also pick up my clothes so my spouse doesn't have to pick up after me.
- In the hall I'll suggest a picture to hang but will check with my spouse to be sure it appeals to my spouse too, in keeping with Ephesians 5:21.
- In the kitchen I'll listen as much as I talk about the day's events in keeping with Ephesians 5:21, 28. We'll do the dishes together. We will share the responsibilities of cooking and shopping.
- In the garage we will have a system for keeping gas in the cars and the lawnmower tuned up. (We may decide that one spouse does the garage work and the other does the cooking and shopping. We'll make that decision together.) We'll do these chores to please God and one another in keeping with Ephesians 5:10.
- In the living room I will plan my next work day while my spouse pays the bills. (Or, we will reverse these roles.) I will help pay for the furniture and wisely shop to get the best quality for the best price in keeping with Ephesians 5:16.

Invite volunteers to tell about one room of their house, citing a verse from Ephesians 5. Stress the delight of seeing each room as a place to show love for your spouse. Close the session by reading Ephesians 5:1, 21, and 31. Thank God for the gift of marriage and the opportunity to build a loving one.

Teacher Tip

As youth map out roles in each room of the house, their minds may turn to sharing sex in the bedroom. This is a good and God-honoring part of marriage that can express love and submission beautifully. Though this session doesn't dwell on it, you should not dismiss it if it is mentioned. Talk honestly with students, reminding them that sex is a wonderful part of marriage and is a gift from God.

EXPECTATION CARDS SESSION 10 — HANDOUT 15

See also pages 111 and 112 for the *Expectation Cards* with a front and back.

 YOU DO THE CLEANING AND OTHER HOUSEHOLD CHORES IN MARRIAGE

 YOU DO THE YARD WORK IN MARRIAGE

 YOU SHOP FOR THE FOOD AND PREPARE THE MEALS IN MARRIAGE

 YOU EARN THE MONEY IN MARRIAGE

 YOU ARRANGE THE HOUSE AND DO THE DECORATING IN MARRIAGE

 YOU KEEP UP WITH RELATIVES, SENDING BIRTHDAY CARDS AND BUYING CHRISTMAS GIFTS, IN MARRIAGE

 YOU TAKE CARE OF THE CHILDREN IN MARRIAGE

 YOU DISCIPLINE THE CHILDREN IN MARRIAGE

YOU PAY THE BILLS IN MARRIAGE

 YOU TAKE OUR KIDS TO THE DOCTOR AND CARE FOR THEM WHILE SICK IN MARRIAGE

Galatians 5:13–15; Hebrews 10:24–25

Do You Roll or Squeeze the Toothpaste?

SESSION 11

Focus on a Goal Truth

It's the little things that make or break a marriage, so choose marriage-making little things such as understanding, kindness, hearing daily events, and gently talking through things.

Understand Concerns Youth Have

- We won't argue about everyday stuff like that because we love each other.
- He drives me crazy with his need for neatness.
- We had a disagreement—does that mean we aren't compatible?

Connect Scripture to Youth Concerns

1. Demonstrate the value of each brick in building—or damaging—a marriage.
2. Recognize two ways to respond to irritating differences.
3. Practice the uniting—rather than dividing—option.

Gather Supplies and Prepare

- Bring extra Bibles, pencils, paper, and masking tape.
- Bring at least 10 sandwich cookies per trio of youth, plus plates on which to build the houses.
- Arrange the chairs in one large circle.
- Photocopy one copy of Handout 16 for each youth.
- Bring extra paper if you decide to use the Bonus Option.
- Photocopy and cut apart several copies of Handout 17.
- Bring paper clips.

SESSION 11

Invite Attention

Step 1:
Build Your House Brick by Brick
(10–15 minutes)

Give trios of youth an equal number of sandwich cookies and a plate. Direct them, **Use your cookies to build a house in the style of your choosing**. Circulate and encourage youth to untwist the sandwich cookies to use the icing as "glue." Make no comment if youth eat or take bites out of the cookies. When building is complete, call for trios to present their buildings, explaining their construction process. Comment positively about unique designs. Ask,

- **How did you style your house? Why did you choose that style?**
- **What held your house together?**
- **Are any of the cookie bricks missing? Who ate them? Why did you eat them?**
- **According to Galatians 5:13–15 how are these houses like a marriage relationship?** Urge all youth to read the verses in their own (or a loaned) Bible. Using students' words, stress the following principles: We were free to do what we wanted with the cookies, but we got a smaller house if we ate them. If we eat at each other, we'll have a smaller and weaker love between us. We were free to eat the cookies but that wasn't the best thing for our house. Working together, we built a strong and sturdy house. There are many styles for a good, strong house.
- **What's the value of each brick in holding a marriage together?** Explain that these bricks are words, attitudes, and actions.

Amid protests of "If you'd told us to build a big house in the first place, I wouldn't have eaten any cookies!" agree that instructions would have helped. Explain, **People who marry frequently think that because they are in love, they need to know nothing more. But knowing a few basic principles can keep you from eating up your love before you can build a lifelong relationship with it. These instructions would include "Keep an eye on the little things" and "Watch the way you talk to each other."**

Dig into the Bible

Step 2: Keep an Eye on the Little Things
(10 minutes)

Guide youth to sit in a large circle. Give these instructions: **When I read a statement, you move one chair to the left if this is true about you. If someone is already in that chair, sit on that person's lap. If two or more people are already in that chair, sit on the top lap. And if you're somewhere in the pile and the statement is true about you, move yourself only.** Sample statements:
- Move to the left if you squeeze the toothpaste rather than roll it.
- Move to the left if you roll toothpaste rather than squeeze it.
- Move to the left if you like your toilet paper to roll over the top of the roll.
- Move to the left if it doesn't matter how it rolls, as long as the paper's there.
- Move to the left if you'd rather eat a sandwich than a meal.
- Move to the left if you'd prefer a hot and hearty meal rather than fast food.
- Move to the left if you're a morning person.
- Move to the left if afternoon is your best time.
- Move to the left if you're a night owl.
- Move to the left if you like being on the go morning, noon, and night.

Say, **Little irritations in a marriage can pile up like you're piled into each other's laps. For example, every time you go to the medicine cabinet and find the toothpaste squeezed in the middle, you wonder why your spouse is so messy. These irritations all stack up to an attack or argument. But you can also think, "Even though we do this differently, we both get the paste out of the tube." Then make a lighthearted joke like, "How's my squeezer today?"** Challenge youth who are still sitting in another lap: **When you tell me a way to understand differences rather than be aggravated by them, you can move to your own chair.** Invite ideas such as the following: Accept differences as long as the differences are not immoral. Do something the other person's way occasionally. Tease without put-downs. Understand the other's point of view. Expect some differences. Consider rolling the toothpaste to give comfort to the other. Take turns eating food the other likes. Let one choose the way you'll both roll the toilet paper and the other choose the toothpaste brand you'll both use.

SESSION 11

Teacher Tip

Take full advantage of the teaching value of this type of game—because youth *did* the activity, they remember its impact. But we must debrief for them to remember the intended purpose—rather than just the fun—of the game. In addition to your comparisons to marriage, invite youth to make comparisons of their own.

Stress, **It's the little things that take apart many marriages and it's the little things that make the good ones strong. Listen again to Galatians 5:13–15, one verse at a time, for tips on how to do the little things that build up a marriage.** Call on a volunteer to read Galatians 5:13 and pause to invite tips. (Examples: Use your freedom to show love. Refuse to indulge yourself at someone else's expense.) Then call on a volunteer to read verse 14 and pause to invite tips. (Examples: Treat my spouse like I want to be treated. Realize the way I treat my spouse reflects on God.) Call on a volunteer to read verse 15 and pause to invite tips. (Examples: Refuse to bite at each other. Watch out that I don't destroy my spouse. Don't let my spouse destroy me. Talk kindly to keep from destroying each other.) Say, **A good marriage boils down to doing the kind and caring action rather than the biting and devouring one. Let your goal in marriage be to do the little things that keep the flame of love alive even when irritation comes.**

Step 3:
Watch the Way You Talk to Each Other
(10 minutes)

Explain that one of the most important little things that builds or harms a marriage is the way we talk to each other. Guide youth, **Give examples of words and tones that would build up a marriage and words and tones that would tear one down.** Use their comments to explain **The way you talk to your spouse is as spiritual as going to church. You either honor or betray God by the way you speak to the people in your house.** Call on a volunteer to read Hebrews 10:24–25. Illustrate it by guiding youth to complete Handout 16, choosing the action/words in each pair that would spur the other on to love and good deeds. Direct youth to keep their Bibles open to Hebrews 10:24–25 as they work. Encourage youth to add at least one more example of a way to encourage through a daily kind action, attitude, or sentence. Invite each youth to pick one pair and demonstrate by tone of voice why the one side is the marriage builder.

Challenge, **Can you name any part of marriage that would not be a spiritual matter, an opportunity to spur the other on toward love and good deeds?** (Example: When your spouse plays a card that loses, say, "We all make mistakes," rather than "Dumb move!") To silly suggestions like "blowing your nose" say, "Well, you could refuse to laugh at the way the other does it, and if one is sleeping you could blow your nose quietly." Then let youth respond to other suggestions with ways to be spiritual. Guide youth to discover that every word, attitude, and action either builds up or tears down the spouse.

Step 4: Gather Your Tools
(10–15 minutes)

Explain, **When there is a problem in a marriage, do we attack the problem or attack each other? Do we show kindness and a kindred spirit, or do we kick at each other in frustration? Paying careful attention to our behavior during problems is an important way to build up rather than tear down our marriage.** Use students' words to emphasize that couples can solve problems if they work at them together, and the strongest couples are those who solve their conflicts, not those who have none. To illustrate this, guide trios of youth to choose at least three tools from Handout 17, which you have photocopied and cut apart to show how to solve a specific problem as a marriage team. Encourage specificity. Ways to use the tools include the following:

- Hammer: Nail down exactly what the problem is. For example, if you're fussing at each other and usually don't, you may be tired and need extra rest. Go to bed early a few nights in a row.
- Screwdriver: Tighten up loose areas on your side of the relationship. For example, if you tend to talk too much, force yourself to listen. If you tend to stay too quiet, force yourself to share your point of view.
- Clamp: Make the relationship solid, caring, and lasting by always doing something together to solve the problem. For example, if the problem is a shortage of money, each give up a purchase you usually make.
- Wedge: Separate yourself from things that cause pain. For example, drive a wedge between you and whining so you can see the good in the situation.
- Wrench: Loosen areas where you've been too tight. For example, you may expect your spouse to be at the supper table at 6:00 and fuss the rest of the evening if he or she is not. Make eating together the focus, not the clock.
- Crowbar: Be firm on removing actions that hurt. For example, if you have a complaint against your spouse, make your spouse the only one you tell it to. This removes your tendency to gossip.
- Glue: Repair mistakes you've made with the glue of forgiveness and a fresh start.
- Sandpaper: Sand off your own rough edges such as a quick temper or ugly words. Smooth your skills of think-before-you-speak and say-loving-words.

Stress, **Each person chooses what tool he or she will pick up and how to use it. The hammer can hurt or bring connection. Choose**

Bonus Option

Guide each youth to fold a sheet of paper in half and tear out a human silhouette. For every letter of their first and last name, have youth write a word or action that one spouse could say to discourage the other.
Sample:

Pitiful example you are!

Angry silent treatment.

Treat him like he's less valuable.

Just complain all the time.

Only speak when I'm upset.

Not once have you done anything right!

Everyone said I shouldn't have married you.

Seems like all we do is fight.

Invite one youth to read Hebrews 10:24–2. Say, **Each time we say or do something ugly, we hurt not only the one we love but ourselves. It's never easy to repair the damage, so it's much better to say and do what loves, encourages, and spurs the other on to good in the first place.** Close by spelling out encouraging words with their names.

SESSION 11

the good use for every tool. Pray for ability to use tools well in problem solving and in all areas of marriage.

Live What You Learn

Step 5: Choose the Little Things (10 minutes)

To review and solidify what youth have discovered about the little things in marriage, direct youth to choose an item from the room—a little thing such as a thumbtack or a piece of chalk—and use it as an object lesson to show that it's the little things that make or break a marriage. Youth can also use items from their purses or pockets. Urge youth to complete this sentence to compose the object lesson:

A happy marriage is like a _____ because … . But it is not like a _____ because …

- A happy marriage is like a thumbtack because we can turn our words to be painful like the pointy end of a thumbtack or comfortable like the rounded end. It is not like a thumbtack because my spouse might not openly bleed when I verbally stab him or her.
- A happy marriage is like a piece of chalk because my actions help write what it becomes, but it is not like a piece of chalk because it's not easy to erase hurtful things I do.
- A happy marriage is like a paper clip because it holds two people together if they're careful not to bend it. A happy marriage is not like a paper clip because it's stronger.

Give each youth a paper clip as a reminder to do the little things that hold a marriage together and work out the little things that divide one. Read Galatians 5:13–15, then read verse 13 again.

HANDOUT 16 — SESSION 11

Encourage!

"How can I help you get your work done while your foot is elevated?"

"Why did you have to go and break your foot now?"

Tell my spouse the yard looks great after the day's work.

Hound my spouse to do the yard work.

"Thanks for sharing the bathroom."

"Why do you take so long in the bathroom?"

Accuse my spouse of not caring when another event conflicts with what I want to do.

Give my spouse notice so there's plenty of time to plan for both events.

"You are so lazy—get up and help me for once."

"When you help with the dishes, we both have more free time."

Tell my spouse the way he or she makes the bed is wrong.

Ask if my spouse will leave extra room for my toes rather than tuck the sheets in supertight.

"I HATE PLAYING WITH YOU—YOU NEVER COUNT YOUR CARDS!"

"We have a good chance of winning if you count your cards."

SESSION 11 — HANDOUT 17

Tool Kit for Marriage Building

Illustrate Hebrews 10:24–25 by showing how this tool could be used symbolically to solve a specific problem as a marriage team. Remember to attack the problem rather than each other.

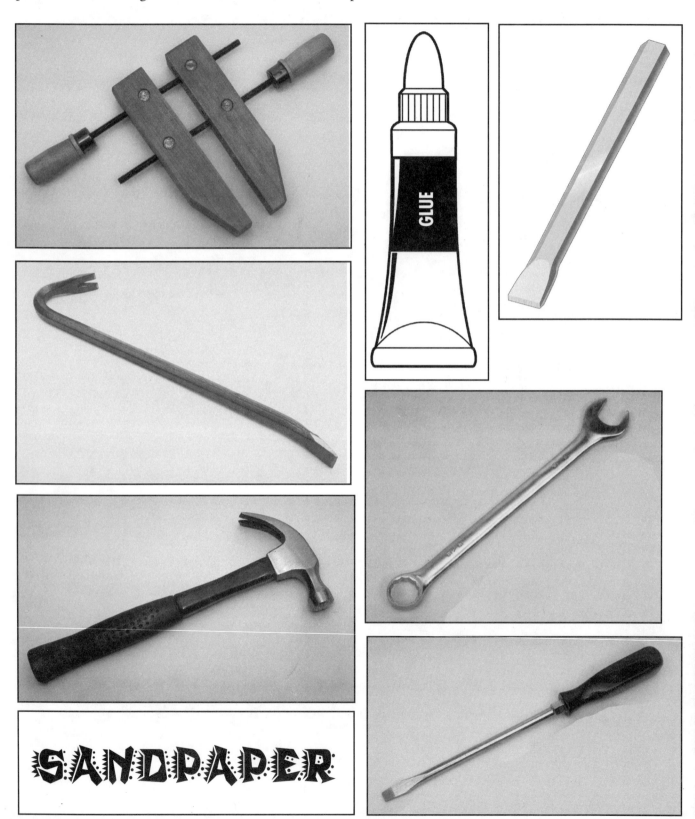

1 John 4:7–21; Matthew 19:4–6

SESSION 12

We're Ready to Commit—Now What?

Focus on a Goal Truth

Work toward a marriage, not just a wedding. Cement and intertwine your relationship daily so you won't want to separate.

Understand Concerns Youth Have

- My wedding day will be the best day of my life!
- Our families disagree on how we should do things. What should we do?
- How can we make sure we don't become a divorce statistic?

Connect Scripture to Youth Concerns

1. Plan a wedding the way it's typically planned.
2. Focus on a Christ-centered marriage that fine-tunes the usual wedding plans.
3. Embrace a wedding as an opportunity to launch caring habits.

Gather Supplies and Prepare

- Bring extra Bibles, pencils, chalk and chalkboard, poster board, and marking pens.
- Photocopy Handout 18 for each youth.
- Arrange for a wedding coordinator to speak if you choose the Bonus Option.
- Bring paper the size of a prescription pad for Step 3.
- Bring an easy-to-blow-up balloon for each youth.
- Bring small paper for bookmarks for Step 5.

SESSION 12

Bonus Option

Invite a wedding coordinator to speak with the youth about common wedding mishaps and how to avoid them. Suggest the coordinator recall couples who enjoyed their wedding days and how they did it. Details to cover include:

- the reason for a rehearsal;
- what if something doesn't go as planned;
- how to manage people who try to tell you what to do;
- how to make a wedding a celebration.

It is important to note that a wedding coordinator is not someone who makes money from how much is purchased for a wedding, but a person who coordinates who stands where and who makes sure things are set up according to the plan. He or she is a neutral figure.

Invite Attention

Step 1: Take Care of Details (10 minutes)

As youth enter, tell them to imagine they have six months to plan their weddings. Direct them to write what they need to do, when to do it, who is responsible for it, and tips for getting it done well using Handout 18. The first four are partially complete to get youth started. For youth who don't immediately jump at this, give them a focus they're interested in. A young boy could plan how to ask his girlfriend's family for permission to marry her. A girl who plans never to marry could focus on the getting-together-of-friends part of a wedding. Direct youth to work in teams of up to four. Point out that Handout 18 gives one planning approach and that youth can be free to develop other approaches.

Ask teams to make their reports. Highlight something wise in each. Then challenge youth, **Pretend you can have only three parts of this wedding plan. What would you keep?** As youth work, point out that they'd seldom have to cut their plan this slim, but it does help them focus on what matters the most to them and to God. As youth report on their slimmed down plans, ask, **Could you narrow this to two things? One thing? Why was it easier to let some things go than other things?** Stress, **The important part of the wedding is the marriage. By keeping a Christ-centered marriage in the forefront we'll make decisions that bring good not showiness.** (Invite youth to name examples such as the following: Make guests feel welcome rather than worry about fancy food. Less fancy arrangements mean more people can come. Dress comfortably to enjoy the day rather than look decorated but be miserable with pinched toes and scratchy clothes. Worry more about coordinating attitudes than colors. See your marriage as a celebration rather than a display. Enjoy the wedding rather than get nervous about each detail. Do the rice run and then come back in and enjoy your company.) Write these on a chalkboard or poster board as youth name them. Tell about a wedding you enjoyed rather than one that was a show. (Sample: The bride had a simple dress and they only had cake at the reception, but I had more fun at their wedding because everyone was laughing and enjoying themselves.)

SESSION 12

Dig into the Bible

Step 2:
Move Weeds So You Can Intertwine
(15–20 minutes)

Say, **A lot of forces will try to get in the way of making your wedding a celebration of marriage. The commercialism of weddings is one—many companies want to make money off your day. Can you name others?** Because many of these competitors don't surface until couples plan a wedding, youth may not know of many. In that event, highlight such areas as the following: There is much to do in very little time. Your own expectations might make you miss the spontaneous good that comes. Family members may want your wedding to go according to their dreams, not yours. Explain that a wedding can be a very stressful time on a new relationship but with deliberate caring action, couples can move past this obstacle. Suggest, **Planning a wedding well is the first step in the many adventures a couple faces: marrying, finding a place to live, working out job schedules, deciding to parent, giving birth to or adopting a baby, raising preschoolers, guiding school-age children, parenting teenagers, making joy in an empty nest, coordinating each stage of life. The couple can either make those things be the happy events they are meant to be or let them cause sadness and stress. It's like a garden—you intertwine with your spouse, but you must pull the weeds of bad attitude and conflict to keep growth strong.** Challenge youth to search 1 John 4:7–21 for actions that make life events good. Youth will cite love; move them to cite specific examples of love in the verse. Write them on the board as youth say them. Samples:

- Be dear friends (v. 7).
- Love one another with the love that comes from God (vv. 7, 11).
- Receive and live God's love (vv. 8–10).
- Show what God is like by the way we treat each other (v. 12).
- Let God's Spirit do loving things through us (vv. 13–16).
- Have confidence that imitating God is right, both now and in the future (v. 17).
- Let love for God and love for my spouse drive out fear (v. 18).
- Let God's love motivate me to love (v. 19).
- Weed out hate for God's sake (vv. 20–21).

Explain, **As you make choices to do the loving thing, even when it's hard, you will build a marriage better than any wedding-day dream. Let's practice.** Give these situations and guide youth to choose an action

SESSION 12

Teacher Tip

Youth tend to give the answer they know their teacher expects. In 1 John 4:7–21 the word *love* appears in nearly every verse, so it is the obvious and very true answer. But your students' understanding will not be complete without understanding what love is and how love acts. Move them further by asking, **With what action will you show love in that situation?** Or, **With what words and tone of voice will you show love in that situation?** Agree that love is not being a doormat but firmly and kindly doing what God would do.

from 1 John 4:7–21 (just written on the chalkboard) that would help. Suggest they write it in prescription form. Then invite youth to name their own starter situations and prescriptions.

You want a big wedding with all the trimmings. Your spouse wants something simple. (Sample: Take one big dose of *Be dear friends (v. 7)* by doing what the other wants. We could have a big, simple wedding—room for lots of people with simple cake and mints, one attendant each.)

Your mother insists on running the show. She wants all the attendants and ushers to wear fancy shoes even though they pinch the toes. You and your fiancé are more interested in celebrating than putting on a show. When you explain this, she says, "It's the only wedding you'll have. I want it to be nice!" (Sample: With a time-release capsule of *Love one another with the love that comes from God (v. 7, 11)* and *Receive and live God's love (vv. 8–10)* we will firmly but kindly refuse her request. This will give the people in the wedding party comfort on a very happy day.)

Your fiancé and you have been arguing a lot during the wedding planning. You feel like eloping to get away from it all. (Sample: Exercise your ability to *Show what God is like (v. 12)*. Instead of running away from the situation, manage it with deliberate kindness. Both of you can *Let God's spirit love through you (vv. 13–16)* by voicing when you feel stressed or confused, and then decide together what to do.)

You returned a wedding gift because you thought you could use something else more. You found out later that your fiancé wanted that gift. You worry that you have hurt your fiancé by neglecting to talk about it first. (Sample: Massage *Love for God and love for my spouse to let it drive out fear (v. 18)*. Apply generously to talking about how your fiancé feels. Ask forgiveness. Consider buying that gift back if possible.)

One relative refuses to come to the wedding if another relative is there. (Sample: Surgically remove hate *for God's sake (vv. 20–21)*. Instead, *Have confidence imitating God (v.17)* by saying repeatedly that we hope each relative will come. We will refuse to play games or let one person pit us against another.)

Reread verses 18–21 to stress that we show love and express emotions well for God's sake.

Step 3:
Cement and Grow Your Relationship
(10 minutes)

Give each youth a balloon and direct all to blow one puff of air in their balloons when any member of the group names a wedding pressure. (Samples: Trying to keep everyone happy, wanting to honor God in every bit of the wedding, getting ready to be a 24-hour-a-day couple rather than a dating one, trying to get the wedding done while working and/or going to school, wondering if all the details will come off well, hoping your cousin will become a Christian through what the pastor says about marriage.)

Stop the balloon blowing when balloons get close to popping size. Direct youth to hold the balloons so no air will exit, and say, **A wedding brings much pressure because it's the start of something new and because many people have expectations for it. Not all pressure is bad—you mentioned wanting to please God with your ceremony. Similar to the way our balloons blow up with pressure, pressure helps us get done what we need to do. But what will too much pressure do?** (Possible answers: Pop the balloon, take away the fun of marriage.) Continue, **We can let pressure out before it pops the balloon, hurts the relationship, or hurts other people. Give me some examples, please.** As youth give examples, cue the group to let a little—but never all—the air out of the balloon. (Examples: Find people who will enjoy the celebration with you. Invite a caring parent or older adult at your church to keep an eye on you and help you keep perspective. Go off by yourself as a couple for a little while. Go off by yourself as a single person for a little while. Spend some time with a friend who cares selflessly for you. Schedule time with the people you want to see during this time so details won't steal your time together. Ask for privacy.) Write these pressure releasers on the chalkboard since they are more important to remember—the pressures will come whether youth remember them or not.

Continue to illustrate by inviting youth to do both pressures and pressure releasers in a way that keeps the balloons about the same size. Suggest, **Some pressures are bigger than others. They might need two or three pressure releasers to take care of them. Some pressure releasers can take care of several pressures. You manage pressure well when you *choose* to show love in the middle of pressure.**

Explain, **These deliberately caring actions not only release pressure, they cement your relationship while allowing room for growth. You cement a relationship by approaching things as a united couple. You grow by listening to truly caring parents and friends who show you how to express a good attitude. This is part of what Jesus urged**

SESSION 12

in Matthew 19:4–6—to grow a relationship so close that you won't want to separate. Invite youth to tell how a friend or date helps them handle pressures. Suggest that this is what to aim for in choosing whom to marry—find someone who helps you handle the pressures, not someone who becomes hateful when pressures come.

Step 4:
Distinguish between Cold Feet and Cold Truth
(5–10 minutes)

Point out that almost every couple wonders if they should go through with getting married. Most of the time this is just normal anxiety over a life-changing event. But sometimes it means the marriage should not take place. Ask, **What's the difference between cold feet that mean you're anxious and cold truth that you should not marry?** After helping youth evaluate the differences they state, stress, **No matter how much you like the other person, and no matter how close it is to the wedding, some things are clear cause for calling the wedding off. These include if your fiancé hits or beats you even once, other indications of physical or verbal abuse, evidence that your fiancé is not willing to build a mutual marriage, not knowing your fiancé's family or background, or the discovery of something suspicious.** Point out that planning a wedding can be a magnifying glass that highlights a serious problem you had not formerly heeded. Pray for God's eyes to see character before the wedding and boldness to follow God's promptings.

Live What You Learn

Step 5:
Crawl Out of the Pits
(10 minutes)

Say, **Now that we have some measure of what to focus on as you prepare to marry, let's discover pitfalls.** Write the pitfalls on the board. Let volunteers explain each pitfall and how they've seen it in real life. Comment on their explanations. Invite youth to name other wedding pitfalls they have seen and ways to climb out of those pits.

- Don't fall into the pit of focusing on the wedding: **Too many people make the day the important part rather than the relationship. When the relationship is the focus, little mishaps in the wedding become fun stories to tell rather than disasters that mess up the day.**

- Don't fall into the pit of leaving too quickly: **Few times in your life bring as many people together as a wedding. Go ahead and run through the rice, and then come back in to visit.**
- Don't fall into the pit of wedding shopping: **Weddings are big business for the wrong reason—greed. Rather than fill merchants' pockets, plan a day that enables friends and loving family to enjoy the start of your marriage.**
- Don't fall into the pit of arguing: **Wedding time can make everybody on edge.**
- Focus on selflessly enjoying each other and the process.

Challenge, **Instead of seeing a wedding as a once-in-a-lifetime launch that has to be perfect, see it as an opportunity to begin habits of caring for your spouse through the easy and hard parts of life.** Review by inviting youth to name a Bible truth they've gained in this session that can teach them loving habits. Or, if this is the last in a series of sessions, invite youth to name an insight from any of the sessions studied. Direct youth to mark in their Bibles 1 Corinthians 13:4–7 or another passage from this series with the bookmark you provide. Stress, **Love is a choice, not a chance. You don't have to wait for Mr. or Miss Right to come along, nor do you have to settle for less than a good match for you. You can make choices and take action to create happy relationships. In the meantime, enjoy life. God will show you how.**

SESSION 12 — HANDOUT 18

Wedding Planner

Treat both your fiancé and every member of your families with the love of God (1 John 4:7–21).

See your wedding as the first of many ways to grow unity between you and your spouse (Matthew 19:4–6).

This is the first day of your marriage, not the only day. Take mishaps as adventures, not disasters. Laugh a lot.

Event/Relationship	Who's Responsible
Commit to each other	Bride and groom
Buy rings	Bride buys groom's and groom buys bride's
List people to invite	
Keep building your relationship as a couple	

Involve people in the wedding in unique ways such as circulating to talk to people at the reception, taking care of your car, entertaining school-age children.

SESSION 12

When to Start/Finish	How Often to Do/ Extra Tips
Before engagement	Daily Tip: _____
_____ _____ _____	Once: Be sure to buy what you have money for now; don't borrow it.
	Tip: Bride and groom ask family members to give names and addresses of the ones they'd like to come. Bride and groom also make their own lists.
	Tip: Ask married couples to give advice for growing through the wedding planning and wedding day.

Remember, the people matter more than the clothes, cake, and colors.

Emotions will be intense around wedding time: Parents will be hoping everything goes well for you but worried that it won't. Friends will want to do well as your attendants. Others will wonder why you didn't ask them to be attendants. You and your fiancé will be hoping you picked the right partner. All this will make the pleasures happier, the irritations more intense. Understand and tread gently.

The wedding is a celebration, not a show.

Many people will have dreams for your wedding. Hear their ideas and then gently but firmly do what you and your spouse-to-be know is best.

- You do the cleaning and other household chores in marriage
- You do the yard work in marriage
- You shop for the food and prepare the meals in marriage
- You earn the money in marriage
- You arrange the house and do the decorating in marriage
- You keep up with relatives, sending birthday cards and buying Christmas gifts, in marriage
- You take care of the children in marriage
- You discipline the children in marriage
- You pay the bills in marriage
- You take our kids to the doctor and care for them while sick in marriage

— Marriage —
Expectations

— Marriage —
Expectations

— Marriage —
Expectations

— Marriage —
Expectations

— Marriage —
Expectations

— Marriage —
Expectations

— Marriage —
Expectations

— Marriage —
Expectations

— Marriage —
Expectations

— Marriage —
Expectations